# MUTINY ON THE ENTERPRISE

"Sir, please do not touch the console." Kirk spun to see several crewmen standing along the rear bulkhead. "Use of the phasers against the society below is wrong."

"Get to your posts immediately. This is a direct order! Lives will be lost if you don't obey."

"We'd like to do as you say, sir, except it means using violence. We cannot do that. Lorelei has explained it all to us."

Kirk didn't have time to argue. He turned to the panel. When the lights flashed ready, he hit the intercom button. "Chekov, fire! I've got the phasers set!"

No answer.

"Chekov, what's happening?"

## Look for STAR TREK Fiction from Pocket Books

Star Trek: The Original Series

*Final Frontier*
*Strangers from the Sky*
*Enterprise*
*Star Trek IV: TVH*
#1 *Star Trek: TMP*
#2 *The Entropy Effect*
#3 *The Klingon Gambit*
#4 *The Covenant of the Crown*
#5 *The Prometheus Design*
#6 *The Abode of Life*
#7 *Star Trek II: TWOK*
#8 *Black Fire*
#9 *Triangle*
#10 *Web of the Romulans*
#11 *Yesterday's Son*
#12 *Mutiny on the Enterprise*
#13 *The Wounded Sky*
#14 *The Trellisane Confrontation*
#15 *Corona*
#16 *The Final Reflection*
#17 *Star Trek III: TSFS*
#18 *My Enemy, My Ally*
#19 *The Tears of the Singers*
#20 *The Vulcan Academy Murders*
#21 *Uhura's Song*
#22 *Shadow Lord*
#23 *Ishmael*
#24 *Killing Time*
#25 *Dwellers in the Crucible*
#26 *Pawns and Symbols*
#27 *Mindshadow*
#28 *Crisis on Centaurus*
#29 *Dreadnought!*
#30 *Demons*
#31 *Battlestations!*
#32 *Chain of Attack*
#33 *Deep Domain*
#34 *Dreams of the Raven*
#35 *The Romulan Way*
#36 *How Much for Just the Planet?*
#37 *Bloodthirst*
#38 *The IDIC Epidemic*
#39 *Time for Yesterday*
#40 *Timetrap*
#41 *The Three-Minute Universe*

Star Trek: The Next Generation

*Encounter at Farpoint*
#1 *Ghost Ship*
#2 *The Peacekeepers*

Most Pocket Books are available at special quantity discounts for bulk purchases for sales promotions, premiums or fund raising. Special books or book excerpts can also be created to fit specific needs.

For details write the office of the Vice President of Special Markets, Pocket Books, 1230 Avenue of the Americas, New York, New York 10020.

# MUTINY ON THE ENTERPRISE

ROBERT E. VARDEMAN

A STAR TREK® NOVEL

POCKET BOOKS
New York London Toronto Sydney Tokyo

This book is a work of fiction. Names, characters, places and incidents are either the product of the author's imagination or are used fictitiously. Any resemblance to actual events or locales or persons, living or dead, is entirely coincidental.

Another *Original* publication of POCKET BOOKS

POCKET BOOKS, a division of Simon & Schuster Inc.
1230 Avenue of the Americas, New York, N.Y. 10020



ISBN: 0-671-67073-5

First Pocket Books printing October 1983

10 9 8 7 6 5



Printed in the U.S.A.

*For the best friends in this or any other universe—*
*Geo. and Lana*

# MUTINY ON THE *ENTERPRISE*

# Chapter One

*Captain's Log,* Stardate 4769.1

> Mapping and preliminary contact of Class Q planet Delta Canaris IV complete. After this mission, the *Enterprise* requires extensive maintenance and the crew sorely needs R and R at Starbase One. I have recommended commendations for several of the crew, notably Mr. Spock for his unflagging efforts in contacting the wafer-thin intelligences on the high-gravity planet. His techniques for contact will establish standards to be used throughout the remainder of our five-year mission and possibly for many years to come by other primary-contact vessels.

"There it is, Captain," came Lieutenant Sulu's excited voice. "Starbase One. It never looked better."

James T. Kirk lounged back in the command seat and stared at the visual display. The orbiting dry docks that would hold a huge starship like the *Enterprise* floated in perfect geometric arrays to one side of the planet. Just a fraction to the right, under the waxy white clouds occasionally laced with the black of storms and the flash of lightning, lay the sprawling complex of Starbase One. Kirk closed his eyes for a moment and vividly remembered the last time he'd been here.

It had been before the start of the *Enterprise*'s current exploratory mission. Before Alnath II and before finding the amazing millimeter-thick intelligences on Delta Canaris. It had been before he had been given command of any ship. As a lieutenant, he had cut a wide swath through the social circles at this starbase. He still remembered some of the long nights, the parties, the excitement.

Kirk sighed and opened his eyes, the memory fading. That was all behind him now. He had more responsibility than anyone should bear. Running a starship the size of the *Enterprise* provided full-time work, full-time worry. Let his junior officers go out and try to match the scrapes he'd gotten into when he had been their age. Kirk knew he'd spend much of his time aboard his ship making certain every piece of equipment got repaired and tuned to the strictest Starfleet standards.

He wouldn't have it any other way.

"Message, Captain," came Uhura's soft voice. "From Admiral McKenna."

Kirk let out a long, low sigh. The last person he wanted to speak with was an admiral, especially one with as hard-nosed an attitude as McKenna's.

"Put the admiral on the screen, Lieutenant," he said. The picture of the planet scrambled and was replaced by a woman, with hair pulled back in a severe style that did nothing to enhance her looks.

"How are you, Admiral?" Kirk greeted.

"Fine, Kirk," she said, her words curt and hard. "Don't bother docking. You won't be in orbit long enough."

"What?" Kirk said, coming fully alert. His eyes narrowed as he studied her. Strands of gray shot through her black hair, adding authority to her looks. The once-fine lines across her forehead and around her eyes had turned into gullies—hard gullies that showed the burdens command placed on her. Kirk wasn't about to let the load ease any on her by shifting duty to him. Not now. Not after the battering his ship and crew had just taken.

"If your ship's doctor rules that you have a hearing impairment, I'll see about removing you from command. Otherwise, prepare to beam aboard a party of three."

"Admiral McKenna, you've had time to examine my status report. This ship requires extensive maintenance work. Our engines need refitting. The computer is long overdue for a checkout available only from a starbase cybernetics expert. My crew is—"

The woman cut him off with a wave of her hand.

"You've put in multiple recommendations for Commander Scott. I've checked his record. He is able to keep any engine running, no matter its condition. Your Mr. Spock trained our head of cybernetics. You report 'excellents' up and down the line, in every department. Have you filed a false status report?"

"Admiral, that's unfair. My crew is the best in space. The *Enterprise*'s record shows that, but we need shore leave. I *demand* it for my crew. They aren't machines able to run forever. They're flesh and blood."

Admiral McKenna ignored Kirk's outburst.

"Look at the ships in dry-dock bays one and four. Tell me what you see."

Kirk leaned back, fingers drumming on the armrest. His eyes never left the screen where the admiral's face peered back at him larger than life. From his station to the right, Spock furnished the information the admiral had requested.

"Those dry docks show starships in total repair conditions. One lacks engines altogether. The other appears to have a large section removed from the bridge area."

"It doesn't have a bridge at all—not anymore." Admiral McKenna's face tightened, her lips pulling back into a thin line hardly more than a razor's slash. "The Romulans saw to that. Blew the *Scarborough*'s bridge, along with Captain Virzi and his officers, into atoms. Commendations went out to four ensigns who assumed command."

"The Romulans?" Kirk asked skeptically. "I hadn't heard of any trouble with them."

"I appreciate your brush with the Klingons. This situation is potentially as dangerous. To the point: there are *no* other starships in even half the condition of the *Enterprise*. There is also no time to waste. This mission will not require battle engagement. I dislike sending you out again without overhaul, but all you are required to do is transport a team of specialists to Ammdon."

"All?" he pressed.

"Almost all. Ambassador Zarv and his peace negotiators will fill you in on any other duties. I've instructed the cargo master in dry dock fourteen to begin loading replacement supplies. If your engineering crew hurries, they might be able to requisition whatever they need to work on your engines while en route to Ammdon."

"Admiral McKenna, I protest your actions. While this situation might be serious—"

"It is, Captain. Ambassador Zarv will brief you. And consider him to be more than just a passenger."

"I'm under his orders?"

"No, Captain Kirk, nothing of the sort. You know that. However," the woman said, clearing her throat, "anything the ambassador *suggests* should be strongly considered to be the next thing to a command. Have I made myself clear?"

"Yes, Admiral."

"Good." For a moment she stared at Kirk, her pale-gray eyes softening a little. "And, Jim, I'm sorry about this. I really am." The picture tore apart and re-formed in the original view of the planet. The white clouds had darkened considerably and gigavolt surges of lightning now racked the leveled mountain where Starbase One rested.

"Captain," came Spock's level voice, "three are beaming up from starbase. Do you wish to meet them?"

"Have we any choice, Mr. Spock?" he asked, a tinge of bitterness in his voice. He glanced up at his science officer and saw one eyebrow lift slightly, the most emotion Spock would show at his balking at orders. "Come on, then. Let's go meet Ambassador Zarv and his team of peace specialists. Mr. Chekov, you have the conn."

The turbo-elevator doors opened and closed, then opened again before Kirk realized he'd left the bridge. His thoughts were as stormy as the thunder racking the planet. His crew deserved shore leave.

"Captain, are you all right?" Spock asked. The Vulcan stood to one side, hands held behind his back.

"Dammit, Spock, I am not all right. She has no right ordering us back into space. My crew needs R and R. This ship needs to be repaired. Even you could use a bit of recreation."

"I, Captain? Hardly." Spock turned and watched the sparkling motes dance around in the transporter beams. The pillars of scintillant energy hardened into figures.

Kirk stepped forward to greet the peace negotiators.

"Kirk?" demanded a short, piglike man. "When can we start for Ammdon? Time is of the essence in this urgent matter. We must not delay. Not an instant!"

"Ambassador Zarv," Kirk said. The Tellarite seemed an unlikely choice for negotiation of any type. He was brusque, rude and going out of his way to be obnoxious. "Welcome aboard the starship *Enterprise*."

"I know what this hunk of tin is!" The transporter technician stiffened. Kirk bit back a smile. Scotty had his engineering section imbued with the same love of the *Enterprise* that he had. If Scotty had heard the *Enterprise* referred to as a "hunk of tin," he'd have heaved the ambassador back into the transporter and dispersed the beam in empty space.

"Then you're aware that we are taking on supplies, that we require certain maintenance, that—"

"Captain Kirk," cut in another of the trio. "Ambassador Zarv is rightfully upset over the delays already encountered in this vexing matter. We need to reach Ammdon as soon as possible, as your superiors have no doubt informed you."

"For what reason do we endanger all our lives?" Kirk asked. The man he addressed appeared to be from Earth. Dressed in a light-blue velvet jacket, frilled dress shirt and tight black breeches, he might have been a fashion model rather than a diplomat. Kirk didn't make the mistake of dismissing him as a fop, however. The man's eyes were chips of polar ice and only the words he spoke were warm. Everything else about him indicated steel under the velvet.

"The planets Ammdon and Jurnamoria occupy adjoining solar systems. Their diplomatic processes are somewhat primitive and lacking compared with ours."

"Get to the point, Lorritson," snapped Zarv. "What he's

trying to say is that these barbarians are going to start shooting at one another unless we intervene. The Federation has a vested interest in maintaining the peace in this region. Mining, manufacturing, all that. Worst of all, Ammdon and Jurnamoria are out in the Orion Arm."

"And the Romulans are making aggressive moves in the area," Kirk finished. He remembered Admiral McKenna's terse comments about the *Scarborough*.

"Precisely. There may be hope for you yet, Captain," said Zarv. When he pulled himself up to his full height, he barely came to the middle of Kirk's chest. Tiny, close-set eyes bored upward, driven by an intensity bordering on fanaticism. "We are experts on the situation, Kirk. Get us there."

Zarv pointed to Spock and said, "You. Take us to our quarters. Now. And get this ship to Ammdon."

Spock glanced to Kirk, who nodded. Spock silently led the ambassador off. Lorritson and the other diplomat remained behind.

"We haven't been formally introduced, Captain," Lorritson spoke up. "I'm Donald Lorritson, chief attaché to the Ammdon system."

Kirk blinked once in surprise. Lorritson was hardly thirty, much too young to hold such a high diplomatic post—unless he was a high-powered negotiator. That made Ambassador Zarv seem all the more capable.

"And the other member of our team is Mek Jokkor. Mek Jokkor's an expert on agricultural products, especially those cultivated in the Orion Arm." Kirk shook hands with Mek Jokkor, felt a slight stickiness when he pulled his hand away. "Mek Jokkor is not animal, such as we are, Captain. No DNA. He is more closely related to the plants of our world than he is to us."

"You don't speak?" Kirk asked, staring openly at the

being. A tiny shake of a human-appearing head was all the answer he got.

"Mek Jokkor's expertise lies in adapting plants of Ammdon for growth on Jurnamoria, and vice versa. He's truly amazing. We are going to use this as a bargaining lever, since much of the problem between the planets deals with food supplies."

A loud cry echoed in the corridor outside the transporter room.

"Thank you for your briefing, Mr. Lorritson," Kirk said quickly. "As much as I'd like to hear more about your mission at this time, I believe your ambassador is . . . bellowing."

Lorritson smiled, then curtly nodded to Mek Jokkor. The pair hurried off, passing Dr. Leonard McCoy in the doorway.

"What's going on, Jim?" McCoy demanded. "What's all the fuss with that Tellarite? And what are they doing aboard?"

"Ambassador Zarv will be more than happy to fill you in, Bones," Kirk said mischievously. "As for myself, I think I've just been pollinated." He wiped the stickiness on his right hand onto his tunic, then left before McCoy asked still another question he didn't want to answer.

"'Tis not possible, sair," Commander Montgomery Scott protested. "Me wee bairns'll nae take the strain." He looked as if he wanted to embrace the powerful engines of the *Enterprise*.

"Do what you can, Scotty. Get as much equipment as possible beamed over while we're in orbit."

"We need dry-dockin'. Nothin' else will do for us."

James Kirk glanced around the engine room. Everything was spotless, gleaming, perfect. No captain in Starfleet had a better engineering officer than Montgomery Scott. Scotty maintained the engines as if the tiniest waggle of an indicator needle from one hundred percent were a nail driven into his own flesh.

"This is going to be a milk run. Nothing too fast. No emergency speeds or maneuvering. All we're doing is taking a three-man diplomatic team to Ammdon."

"Ammdon!" cried the engineer. "That's on the other side of the universe!"

"Not quite," said Kirk, smiling. "But the ship will hold together, won't it?"

"Aye, that it will," said the engineer with some regret. Kirk saw that Scotty wanted to rip into the engines and lovingly rebuild them from scratch, to make them even more powerful, to give them just a bit more performance. "But I canna recommend it."

"What's the worst that can go wrong?"

"The magnetic bottles. The fields get mighty thin in places. One rupture and we lose all power. We might nae survive that, sair." Scotty made an expressive gesture with his hands showing everything blowing apart.

Kirk thought that over, then asked, "What warp factor do you consider a safe maximum? Other than impulse power over to a dry dock?"

"Well, sair, nothin' beyond warp factor three. The strain . . ."

"I know, Scotty. How well I know." Kirk took a deep breath, scanned the engine room once more, then said, "Carry on. And I'll try not to ask more than warp two."

"I dinna mean it was all right to go even that fast, sair. I meant to say that warp three is the max."

Kirk left Scotty mumbling to himself, fiddling with dials and making volumes of notes on new and different ways of fine-tuning the precious engines. Still, Captain Kirk worried over the instability in the magnetic bottles in the warp engines. The powerful magnetic fields held in the colliding matter and antimatter that thrust the ship through warp space. The slightest weakening of that field meant loss of power at best and total destruction at worst.

Then Kirk put it out of his mind. He had his orders. Let Scotty carry out his.

"Status report, Mr. Chekov."

"All fine, Captain," the navigator responded. "On course, warp factor two, as ordered."

"Spock?" he asked. "What's ship's status?"

"The computer checkout is proceeding according to schedule, sir. It employs a new program I wrote for just this purpose."

"You wrote it in your spare time, I assume, Mr. Spock?"

"Of course, Captain." Spock sounded almost indignant. "I would never take time from duty to work on a personal project such as this."

Kirk shook his head and settled into the command seat. During the three weeks since leaving Starbase One, the *Enterprise* had functioned perfectly. Only the presence of the diplomats aboard shattered routine. And Ambassador Zarv did all he could to make everyone in the crew feel as if they were personally responsible for preventing him from reaching Ammdon and the peace conference. Kirk had spoken with Donald Lorritson about the ambassador's attitude, but Lorritson had offered little consolation.

"Ambassador Zarv," he'd said, "is a man obsessed. He sees the danger in any war in the Orion Arm. If the Romulans intervene, we either lose all contact with the free planets scattered along the arm or we launch an interstellar war. Zarv is an adroit negotiator, one of the best in the Federation. Just put up with him for a few more days."

Kirk hadn't liked the suggestion but had no other course of action. The ambassador's constant harping on the slowness of the ship distracted the crew from their duties and reinforced the anger at not being allowed shore leave.

"Mr. Spock, since this is a relatively unmapped region of space we're crossing, have all the appropriate crew make accurate records for future use. The *Enterprise* ought to be more than a taxi service, after all. When we return to Starbase One, I want to show Admiral McKenna complete charts of our course."

"The mapping is already under way, Captain. I took the liberty of ordering it to keep the crew occupied."

"Good." Kirk slumped back in the command seat, eyes dancing from one control console to the next. Sulu's work at the helm was precise, perfect. But then there was scant reason for it to be anything else. Besides being capable, the Oriental helmsman had little to do. The course had been locked in and then forgotten. Only dreary, gas-cloud-littered space reached out in all directions from the ship. Pavel Chekov took the time to make practice runs with the phaser crew, shaving fractions of seconds off their response time. Spock worked with his computer. Uhura daydreamed, her services as communications officer unneeded for at least another week. Even then, contact with Ammdon would be by the book and routine.

Routine. All around him was nothing but routine. And he was bored.

The flashing of alarm lights and the siren running up and down the scale jerked him away from his thoughts.

"Spock, report!" he snapped.

"Unidentified vessel off the port side, Captain."

"No voice or visual contact, sir," came Uhura's quick words.

"Deflector shields at one-half power."

"Aye, aye, sir." Chekov quickly changed from drill to reality. "What about phasers, sir?"

"Power up, but hold your fire."

"Captain, the ship is adrift, powerless, a derelict. But I detect faint life-form readings. Correction, I detect one life form of an unusual nature."

"Explain."

Spock looked up from his scope and shook his head. "I cannot. The life-form reading does not conform to any recorded in our data banks. Also, the ship design is unknown."

"Sulu, plot a vector parallel to the derelict." Kirk stabbed one of the com buttons on his seat arm. "Transporter, ready to beam aboard one life form of unknown species." Another quick jab of the com button. "Dr. McCoy to the transporter room. Bring full alien medic gear." Before McCoy could respond, Kirk had punched several more command buttons.

He reveled in the action. He wasn't bored any longer. The *Enterprise*'s mission wasn't to ferry obnoxious diplomats; it was to explore the unknown, to find and contact new life forms.

"This mission might actually prove worthwhile," he said, more to himself than anyone else.

The opening and closing of the turboelevator door behind him gave him a few seconds to prepare for the verbal onslaught he knew was coming.

"Kirk, what's the meaning of this outrage?" bellowed Zarv. "We can't take the time to go scurrying off to poke into odd corners. Ammdon and Jurnamoria are at each other's throats *now*. I need to be there to stop them. I need to be there to stop the Romulans!"

"Ambassador Zarv," Kirk said, his voice low and calm, "we cannot abandon that ship. You, as a Federation expert on space law, ought to know that a distress signal takes precedence over any other mission. *Any* other one."

"Distress signal? What distress signal? Was there any

radio communication?" Zarv turned and poked a chubby hand at Uhura. "You there. What signal?"

"A life-form reading is sufficient for a rescue mission, Captain," Spock pointed out. "We are in the process of beaming the sole survivor of this disaster aboard."

"He might carry a space plague. We might all die. Then I'd never reach Ammdon. By the Antares Maelstrom, I've got feebleminded peasants all around me. All around!" The ambassador threw his stubby arms in the air and stalked off the bridge.

"Mr. Spock, let's see what we've beamed aboard. Mr. Chekov, you have the conn."

In the transporter room, Dr. McCoy already bent over a tiny form. All Kirk saw was a light fluttering of a diaphanous sea-green material until he moved around for a better look.

The woman's eyes fluttered open and locked on his. James Kirk took an involuntary step forward, his hand lifting to reach out to her.

"She's in shock, Jim. I think."

"What, Bones? Oh, yes. Shock. Aren't you certain?"

"I'm only a doctor, not a mind reader. Outwardly, she looks human enough."

"I'll say."

"But look at the medical tricorder readings." He held up the device for Kirk's inspection. The flashing lights all indicated severe problems—for a human. "She's alive, and she shouldn't be. Heavy radiation exposure, yet she's alive. No indication of a significant metabolic rate, yet she's warm."

"Warm," Kirk said in a distracted tone. His eyes never left hers. A tiny smile curled at the edges of her lips and a light blush graced her cheeks. "She's lovely."

"Help me get her to sick bay. Maybe I can find out more then."

"There is no need, Dr. McCoy," she said. Her voice came light and airy, a spring breeze caressing tall pines. "While I am not entirely healthy, I shall live."

"How is it you speak our language?" McCoy demanded. "I checked your bioreadings through the ship's computer, and the Federation has never found a race such as yours."

"I . . . learn languages quickly. All languages." She sat up, smoothing the thin gown about her slight figure. She leaned forward and looked once again into Kirk's eyes. "The spoken languages are the easiest to master. The unspoken ones are much more difficult."

"What happened to your ship?" Kirk managed to ask.

She shrugged. "A mechanical malfunction. The crew all perished. I know little of starships. I am a Speaker."

"A speaker? From what planet?"

"I am native to Hyla."

Kirk looked up at Spock, who shook his head. "That planet's unknown to us. Can you give us more information about it?"

"Certainly, though my knowledge of location is limited. I have been alone aboard the *Sklora* for almost two months. During much of that time, our engines fired at random. When the fuel ran out, the *Sklora* continued on its last vector."

"So you don't know where Hyla is?"

"I do not know where we are now."

"Jim, dammit, can't you see she's been through a lot? Stop grilling her like she was a spy. I need to do a full bio on her."

"Please, Doctor, believe me when I state I am relatively uninjured. I am in no danger."

Her gaze again went to Kirk.

"Do you have a name?" the captain asked. "Calling you Speaker seems a bit . . . distant."

"Yet these friends of yours call you Captain." She smiled and took any sting from the words. "We do not have names such as McCoy and Spock and Kirk."

"So we call you Speaker."

She smiled, and Kirk almost melted in its radiance. "Call me Lorelei."

# Chapter Two

*Captain's Log,* Stardate 4801.4

The trip so far has been routine, except for the rescue of Lorelei, Speaker of Hyla. Spock has examined our computer records carefully and has found no indication such a planet exists. However, McCoy is certain Lorelei's biopatterns are approximately Terra norm. The differences that do exist do not preclude her from breathing our atmospheric mix or eating our food. She is a striking woman, intelligent, pretty and possessing some undefinable quality I find compelling.

I wish Ambassador Zarv had a fraction of this charm.

Fat blue sparks arced from the control panel to the terminals on the warp engines. One technician was caught between. The smell of burned flesh permeated the engine room even as his agonized screams died to soft moans.

"Get McCoy down here on the double," Scotty yelled. "The engines. Cut back on power ten percent. You, McConel, get the lead out. I need a computer readin' before shuttin' down entirely."

The red-haired crew chief hurried about her mission while Scott gently moved the injured technician away from the short circuit. The engineering officer was oblivious to the sparks just fractions of an inch above his head as he grabbed limp forearms and started pulling. Only when the man was entirely away from the panel did Scotty sit back on the deck plates and heave a sigh.

"Me engines. Me precious wee engines." He shook his head. The arc built in intensity, rising up like a rainbow bridge of death between control panels and engine casing. Already, blackened metal turned to slag and began to puddle on the deck. Intricate printed circuit boards, integrated cubics and wiring exposed to the heat smoldered, too, and began to char. In another few seconds, the matter-antimatter exciter circuits would be ruined.

"Got it, Scotty," the redhead yelled from across the engine room. "Kill the power on twenty-three."

"But, lass, that'll shut off life support over half the ship!"

"I call 'em as I see 'em," came the immediate reply.

Scott didn't hesitate to give the order. Better to leave much of the *Enterprise* without lights and air for a few minutes than to allow the engine to explode.

"What's going on, dammit?" came Dr. McCoy's querulous demand for information. "You shut off all the power in the corridors. The doors won't even open."

"Sorry, Doctor, but I'm a-needin' your medical help before givin' explanation."

"Why didn't you say so?" McCoy dropped beside the

technician, made a face, then glanced up at Scotty. "Third-degree burns over his shoulders and back. Electrical?"

"Aye, that they are." The fiery arc had vanished as quickly as it had come after Scotty ordered the powering down of control bus twenty-three.

"Not much I can do for him here. He needs isolation. Burn gel. Plasma. Some touch-up surgery on these veins and arteries." Even as he spoke, McCoy worked. His medical tricorder gave the weakened vital-sign readings while he injected a beta-endorphin stimulator to ease the man's pain.

"Here's a medical team, Doctor," Chief McConel said. She motioned for the litter bearers to get the injured man on immediately. They jockeyed the antigrav platform down beside him, carefully scooped up the technician and had him floating out to the sick bay in less than a minute.

"Anymore, Scotty?" asked McCoy.

"Nae more, Doctor, praise be. Andres is the only one."

Leonard McCoy glanced around, then shrugged. "I'll do what I can, but don't find a spare to replace this one when I fix him. I don't like to be rushed."

"Report, Chief," ordered Scotty. "What's happened?"

"Not as bad as it looked. The exciter circuit can be rebuilt. Might cut our power a wee bit until then, but nothing we canna handle."

Scotty beamed at his chief. It was good having someone who cared for the engines as much as he did. It was even better that she was Scottish, too.

"Commander Scott, status." Scotty turned to see Captain Kirk swing through the partly opened door. The control circuits for the doors were doubled with the life support throughout much of the ship. "I need power to decks four through eight."

"Captain, it's as I told you. I kenna when we'll be back to normal."

Kirk's sharp eyes darted about, located the malfunction immediately and studied the damage.

"It's not too bad, Captain," Chief McConel answered his unspoken question. "But the magnetic bottles on the starboard engine thin down perilously close to rupture point."

"Is that what caused this? The magnetic field thinned and allowed radiation seepage?"

"The circuits overloaded trying to stabilize, sair." Scotty gestured, his agitation visible. "We canna do more than we're doin' now."

"If I reduce speed to warp one, will that help you get repairs under way?"

"It'd be better, sair, if we found a dry dock. I need shielding to properly work on the engines." Scotty's pained expression told Kirk that this wasn't a meaningless plea. His chief engineering officer meant every word.

"We're still some fifteen days' travel from Ammdon. Dropping speed makes it even longer. You know why we have to get the diplomatic team there, Scotty. Do what you can. Keep the engines running."

"Aye, sair. I can keep them a-runnin', but not safely."

"Do whatever you have to, Scotty. I have faith in you." Kirk turned to leave, then hesitated and spoke to Chief McConel. "Heather, do you have the still in the biology lab on deck four?"

"Sair!" she protested, straightening up and locking her green eyes directly on his. " 'Tis against regs to run a still."

"Oh, I see. Well, it has been my experience that a power shortage tends to cause the mash already in a still to cool. This reduces yield and quality."

"Sair!"

"I don't care about yield, but everything aboard the *Enterprise* must be quality. Carry on."

James Kirk smiled briefly, then hurried for the sick bay.

"I don't know, Bones," Kirk said, leaning back in the chair and sipping at the brandy the doctor had given him. "It looks as if this mission is turning sour."

"If you mean the technician who almost got himself electrocuted—and who you see is doing fine under my care—that's the sort of thing that happens all the time aboard a starship."

"All the time, Bones? Not aboard the *Enterprise*."

"You know what I mean. If you go messing around with currents and all that, you have to expect to get burned once in a while."

"Still distrustful of machines? And what did you do for him? No," Kirk said, holding up his hand. "Let me guess. You plopped him down on a bioscan table and let the computer analyze his every internal function and level. Then you ran a graphics probe over his body and let the computer match it with the way he appeared before the burns. A little hocus-pocus with automated surgery, a bit of reconstruction done via holographic imaging, then you placed him in the gentle care of the sick-bay monitoring computer."

"You've made your point," McCoy said sourly. "But that still doesn't mean I like machines. Taking over everywhere. Everywhere." McCoy took a stiff drink, made a face, then poured himself another two fingers' worth of the potent liquor.

"What I meant about the mission turning sour was Zarv and the others. They pace the halls. They seem to go out of their way to antagonize the crew."

"I expect it of someone like Zarv. He has all the personality of a boar in rut. But that Lorritson. He seems like a nice enough fellow. Knew a guy who looked a lot like him. Farmer, back in Georgia."

"Ah, now we get all bucolic," Kirk said, smiling. "But I think you've got Lorritson wrong. There's something very hard about him. About Zarv, too. I don't think the powers that be in the Federation sent them on their mission without reason. There's nothing that says we have to like them, though."

"I like that Mek Jokkor fellow. Never says much."

Kirk looked at McCoy, then saw that the doctor didn't know about the alien's background.

"About all I know about him is that he cringes whenever anyone eats broccoli in the mess."

"Strange phobia," mused McCoy. "Must go back to his childhood."

"No doubt."

For a while the two sat and drank in silence, their thoughts private. Then came the disturbing sounds of an argument out in the corridor.

"I wish you'd see to soundproofing the sick-bay walls," McCoy complained. "I have to put up with this all the time."

"Quiet, Bones. Listen."

"So now you're spying on your own crew? Where will it end?" he asked in mock disgust.

"Listen, I said."

The voices rose in pitch and fervor. One said, "The bottles are going. I know it. The whole ship's going to explode."

"The captain's crazy," came a second voice. "He's leading us straight into the middle of a war."

"What's the difference if we all die in a matter-antimatter explosion?" demanded the first.

Kirk rose to his feet and said quietly, "This gets nipped in the bud right now."

McCoy shrugged and watched as Kirk opened the door and stepped into the corridor.

Two crewmen leaned against the bulkhead, arguing with one another. When one saw Kirk, he fell silent, then tugged at the other's sleeve and motioned.

"Very good, gentlemen," Kirk said in a controlled voice. "I couldn't help overhearing your wild conjectures and misinformed opinions about the condition of this vessel."

"You're going to kill us. It's wrong to waste our lives like that," blurted one, an ensign.

"What? Who's killing whom? No one's dead. A technician was injured in an accident, nothing more. Dr. McCoy assures me Chief Andres will be healed in another few days."

"You're trying to kill us. That's wrong."

"What do you mean, mister?" snapped Kirk. "What makes you think I'm trying to kill anyone? You're part of this crew and you shall act like it at all times. Do I make myself clear?"

"Aye, aye, sir," said the second. Fear coated his words like a heavy syrup. He backed away from Kirk as if he'd caught his captain with a bloody murder weapon in hand.

"He'll kill us all," murmured the first. "I know it. Look at him. His eyes. A killer!"

"Once more. Attention!" Kirk barked. Both men braced. "You two are both on duty. I trust you have not been imbibing too heavily of Chief McConel's rocketwash at any time—and not at all while on duty."

"We're not drunk, sir."

"You're not acting in a manner that disproves it. Both of you are on report for insubordination and lack of courtesy to a senior officer. Mr. Spock will assign your punishment details."

Both waited for Kirk to turn and stalk back into McCoy's

office. Only when the door slid shut behind him did James Kirk relax.

"I heard, Jim. What's going on?"

"I don't know, Bones. Never have I encountered that kind of reaction. Disobedience, but it seems to be . . . different." He went to the doctor's desk and flipped the intercom. "Bridge? Good, let me speak to Spock."

In a moment came the Vulcan's level tones. "How may I aid you, Captain?"

"Information. Are Spacemen Bretton and Gabriel currently on duty?"

"They are, Captain," Spock replied without hesitation. "Both have been assigned to aid the alien Lorelei in whatever way they can."

"Lorelei?"

"She is being shown how to use the ship's computer library and other facilities, such as the mess, the gymnasium equipment and other devices unknown to her."

"Lorelei," Kirk repeated.

"That is correct, Captain."

"Are those the only two in direct contact with her?"

"Unknown, sir. I assume they have introduced her to many in the crew. Is something wrong?"

"I . . . don't think so. Thank you, Mr. Spock." Kirk switched off the intercom and stared at McCoy. "At least, I hope nothing's too terribly wrong."

"As you were," Kirk said as he swung into the wardroom. His senior officers had risen from the table to stand at attention. Only the three diplomats remained seated. He took his seat at the head of the table, switched on the recording computer and nodded to Ambassador Zarv.

"Good," the pig-faced man said in a harsh, grating voice. "You decide to come, after all."

"I was delayed by ship's affairs, Ambassador. You requested this briefing session. Please get on with it."

"Briefing session?" Zarv cried. "This is nothing of the sort. This is a demand for more speed! We must reach Ammdon without further shilly-shallying about."

"What the ambassador is saying, Captain," spoke up Donald Lorritson, "is that the reduction in speed is not acceptable at this time."

"Not acceptable, Mr. Lorritson? To whom?"

"To Federation leaders, Kirk!" bellowed Zarv. He rose and pounded pudgy hands against the table.

Kirk looked up and down the officers sitting at the table and saw varying degrees of disgust, amusement and horror at the outburst. Uhura managed to look the most shocked that anyone would speak to her captain in such a tone. Sulu's expression mingled amusement and disdain. McCoy was about ready to boil over. Something about Zarv irritated the doctor considerably. Even Spock twitched slightly. Kirk would have to ask about the Vulcan's apparent discomfort at the outburst.

"The *Enterprise* has not been in dry dock for repairs, Ambassador," he said slowly. "As a result, equipment malfunctions more than it would under optimal conditions."

"You can't warp into the Ammdon system looking like you're falling apart!"

"Why not? My orders are to deliver you and your party, nothing more." But Kirk knew there was something more. He remembered Admiral McKenna's comment to that effect.

"Captain," said Lorritson, clearing his throat. "A strong presence is required for this mission. A *strong* one by the *Enterprise,* if you catch my drift."

"Mr. Lorritson, I do not. The admiral knew this ship was not up to fighting trim when she dispatched us. Are you implying we are required to carry out military action once in the Ammdon system?"

"No, nothing of the sort, nothing of the sort!" the man protested. "Rather, let us say that the appearance of strength is more important than firepower."

"You," said Spock, "are using the *Enterprise* as a lever in your bargaining with Jurnamoria. If we appear to enter on Ammdon's behalf, you feel Jurnamoria will give in to your demands."

"Crudely put, but adequate enough in this context."

"That means Spock hit it right on the nose," mumbled McCoy. "They're using us as a clay pigeon in a shooting gallery."

"Kirk, we need speed. Two weeks to get to Ammdon is out of the question. It must be days. This is a starship. Push it to warp factor eight. Do it now. I order it!"

"Ambassador Zarv, you are not captain of this ship. And if you were, you'd realize how suicidal that course of action would be. My engineering officer is not present at this meeting because he is busy at work repairing damage already caused by cruising at a speed we consider hardly more than a snail's pace. Mr. Scott is, bar none, the best engineer in Starfleet; he has said our engines will not maintain warp three, much less warp factor eight."

"Fire him. Put this . . . this Vulcan in. He knows how to make the engines work." Zarv pointed a stubby finger at Spock. The only response was a slightly elevated eyebrow and the beginning of a dyspeptic expression on Spock's sallow face.

"While our officers are capable of performing in different positions, I prefer to leave the specialists alone. Scott is a specialist, as is Spock. They are doing quite well where they are."

Zarv sputtered and stood up so quickly his seat toppled

to the deck. He stormed from the wardroom without a backward look. Lorritson and Mek Jokkor glanced at one another. The plant man followed his superior, leaving Lorritson behind.

"Zarv is not the easiest being in the galaxy to get along with, Captain," explained Lorritson. "But try to understand the scope of this mission."

"I intended this to be a briefing. Would you do us the honor, Mr. Lorritson?"

The man took a deep breath, then let it out. He rose, brushed nonexistent lint off his purple Altairan linen jacket, squared his shoulders and settled into an orator's stance.

Kirk watched in fascination as Lorritson turned from a harried underling into someone dynamic, powerful, dominant.

"The Romulan Empire borders on the systems of Ammdon and Jurnamoria. They have been making minor incursions into Federation space for many months. Nothing serious, not until the *Scarborough* incident. This convinced the Federation leaders that the Romulans had finally decided to make their bid for several planets here and here and here." Lorritson turned on the computer's holo display showing the Orion Arm. The planets he pointed out began to flash for emphasis.

"This gives them a wedge through our occupied area. We stand to lose much in the way of mineral deposits, not to mention—immediately—a dozen inhabited planets."

"The plan appears logical," Spock said. "The Romulans gain valuable area with minor risk to them. This region is too distant for the Federation to patrol adequately."

"Correct, Mr. Spock," agreed Lorritson. "The Federation cannot do it, but Ammdon and Jurnamoria together can. While the two planets are more primitive than most in the

Federation, they have the advantage of being strategically located."

"With Federation aid, they can deter the Romulans. Is that it?" asked McCoy. "You get peace between Ammdon and Jurnamoria; then the Federation supplies both with weapons of war."

"Something like that, Doctor. While we never like to see war, this particular one might prove disastrous for the Federation for many decades to come. You can begin to understand some of the frustration Ambassador Zarv now feels at our delay."

Kirk studied the hologram and let his soldier's mind work on the details. He saw nothing amiss with what Lorritson had outlined. If the Romulan Empire succeeded in establishing a beachhead in the Orion Arm where the diplomat said, fighting would be long and bloody. Better to prevent the small war between two planets than allow the greater one between entire civilizations.

"I see Zarv's reason for impatience, but I made no idle comment about the *Enterprise*'s condition. We can run at warp one without difficulty. Warp two poses problems. Warp three is out of the question until we orbit a planet with sufficient shielding and equipment to perform a major overhaul."

"Is there no way at all to squeeze just a little more speed from your starship, Captain?" This was the closest Lorritson had come to pleading.

"I'm afraid not. The laws of physics are inviolable. We shall get you to Ammdon as soon as possible. I'm sure it won't be fast enough for any of our tastes." Kirk made a wry face when he heard Zarv's bellowing out in the corridor.

"Do your best, Captain. The ambassador, Mek Jokkor and I must put the final touches on our presentation."

Lorritson folded a few papers in front of him and quickly left.

Spock indicated the desire to speak. Kirk motioned for him to begin.

"The diplomats have used the ship's computer for extensive games-theory plays to examine all possible outcomes. While I had no intention of spying, my certification of the computer required certain tests which divulged information."

"So you were spying, Spock. Go on. Give us the juice. What did you find?" McCoy leaned forward, eager for the gossip.

"I resent your implications, Doctor." Spock stared straight ahead as he reported, "If Mek Jokkor's projections about food levels are accurate—and I have no way of checking the basic assumptions—the diplomatic team will succeed in their mission. In spite of personal friction I've witnessed with crew members, they are admirably suited for this delicate mission."

"Thank you, Mr. Spock." Kirk looked around the table. "If there are no other comments, this briefing is adjourned." He didn't like the lackluster way his officers left the room, almost as if they'd been handed their death sentences.

"Captain Kirk, may I have a word with you? In private?"

Kirk turned to see Lorelei whirl around the corner of the corridor, a puff of mist floating on the wind. As her chocolate eyes met his, he felt his heartbeat quicken. Something about the way she looked at him affected him like a first love, a forbidden romance, a stolen kiss.

"Certainly. What is it you need? Has the crew been treating you well?"

"Very well, Captain—James." The way she said his name sounded like a lover's whisper. Kirk shook himself to break the image forming in his mind. It was pleasurable but only a fantasy.

"My quarters are nearby. Please join me for a drink."

"I do not like your alcohol, but your coffee stimulates me."

Once in his quarters, Kirk sat behind his desk, feeling like a defender in a fortress. For once he was glad the massive wooden surface separated him from the pretty woman. He watched Lorelei over the rim of his glass, trying to decide if she was really pretty or not. She had even features, translucent skin with a faint nut tinge to it, soft brunette hair and those wide-set brown eyes that pulled him in every time he looked at her.

Pretty, no, he decided. Comely, perhaps. Attractive. Definitely attractive.

"Captain, I have listened to your crew, talked with some of them. I am worried about the safety of the ship."

"The ship? You mean the accident in the engine room? Put it out of your mind. It was unfortunate, but the technician is recovering nicely. Our medical facilities are excellent."

"I do not mean the injury, although that is serious. I refer to the danger you place the *Enterprise* in by journeying to the Ammdon system."

"What do you know of that?"

"The ship's computer records are most complete, and I am not without some native reasoning ability."

He frowned at the small woman. "I'm sorry we can't take you back to Hyla immediately, but our mission is a peaceful one. We go to prevent war in the Ammdon system, not cause one, as you implied."

"Your presence will initiate the war. The rulers of Ammdon will use your presence to launch a preemptive strike against Jurnamoria."

"For someone who didn't even know the Federation existed until we rescued you, you've got a lot of notions about how things work."

"I know the nature of reasoning beings. We are all violent, Captain. Violence has allowed us to survive our primitive beginnings. But no longer do we need to kill one another. Other, more peaceful challenges exist for us. You cannot enter the Ammdon system without endangering the welfare of your *Enterprise*."

Kirk felt his hands begin to shake slightly. He carefully placed his glass on the desk in front of him.

"I must trust my superiors and their assignment of Zarv and the others to this peace talk. They are capable."

"Ammdon uses you."

"Explain." Kirk had meant to snap out the word, a command. He found himself hesitating, almost not wanting to hear Lorelei's explanation, because he knew it would go against all he believed.

"Ammdon and the Federation have a mutual defense treaty. The Federation and Jurnamoria do not. In any war, Ammdon expects Federation backing."

"How do you know of this treaty?"

"It is recorded in your computer."

He swallowed hard as he punched up the information. The digest of the treaty confirmed what Lorelei had said.

"If you enter the system, this will give Ammdon the opportunity to attack. You will start the war, not prevent it."

Kirk felt himself adrift in a sea of conflicting emotions. Lorelei spoke persuasively, logically. Yet Zarv and Lorritson and Mek Jokkor were trained professionals. They did not want war; they wanted only peace. They'd do nothing to jeopardize the Federation's position in the Orion Arm. The constant threat of the Romulans was too real.

"I—" he began.

"James," Lorelei said, her voice low, a vibrancy about it that reached into his soul and tugged. "You endanger your ship, your crew and the lives of people on two planets. Do not carry through with your orders. Return to Starbase One."

"Lorelei, I can't," he managed to say. She lowered her head, nodded, then left his quarters. He felt as if he'd just accidentally set his cat on fire.

The burden of command weighed heavily on James T. Kirk as he sat in his quarters, staring at a blank wall and mulling over what both Lorritson and Lorelei had said.

War? Or peace? Both were within his power to cause or avoid. One wrong decision—one right decision. Whom was he to believe?

# Chapter Three

*Captain's Log,* Supplemental

> The Speaker of Hyla, Lorelei, troubles me strangely. I find myself increasingly convinced by her arguments to abort the peace mission to Ammdon and Jurnamoria and return to Starbase One. The condition of the *Enterprise* continues to deteriorate. Equipment malfunctions are the least of our problems. My greatest concern is the crew upset and growing disaffection. It is almost as if the crew is on the brink of disobedience, but that is absurd. Such a thing cannot happen on this ship. It will not.

"Explain more fully, Mr. Spock." James Kirk watched as his science officer lifted one thin eyebrow, giving him a slightly perplexed—or offended—aspect.

"My report was clear enough, Captain. Dr. McCoy and Mek Jokkor disrupted the wardroom with their argument. The crew observing this imbroglio became most agitated and many failed to report to their duty stations afterward."

Kirk frowned. None of this made the least sense to him, but it would. Soon. He'd get to the bottom of this if it was the last thing he did.

"Mek Jokkor cannot speak. How did McCoy manage to have an argument with a plant creature lacking vocal cords?"

Spock peered down his nose at his superior. "The computer console is quite capable of accepting an alien's input and translating it into voice readout even Dr. McCoy can understand."

"So not only McCoy but all the crew in the wardroom heard Mek Jokkor's outburst. Punch it up on the computer. I want a replay." Spock silently obeyed. Kirk locked his fingers behind his back and rocked to and fro as he worked over the problems in his mind. The friction between his staff and that of Ambassador Zarv had been limited to minor squabbles prior to this. He'd have to take McCoy to task for upsetting the delicate balance of protocol that had been established.

". . . you are wrong, animal human," came the computer-simulated voice of the alien. "This mission is vital to the Federation's security. A peaceful Ammdon-Jurnamoria system yields stability, both in human terms and against the aggressive Romulans."

"Our presence will cause the war, I tell you," came McCoy's aggrieved voice. "Ammdon will use the *Enterprise* as a tool of war, not of peace. They're going to make damn fools of us over this dispute; they're making fools of the entire Federation."

"But—" Kirk started, then bit off his sentence.

"Yes, Captain?" Spock looked at him squarely.

"Nothing. It's just that I have heard similar sentiments recently. McCoy does not appear to be alone in his thinking. Or perhaps I'm wrong. Maybe the wheel has been reinvented."

"I do not understand."

"Nothing, Spock. Continue with the recording." Kirk only half-listened to the argument carried on via computer between his ship's doctor and the ambassador's aide and agricultural expert. The words changed slightly with McCoy interpreting them, but, on the whole, the arguments carried precisely the same content as those he'd heard so recently from Lorelei.

Lorelei.

Kirk sighed, thinking of the woman, her allure, the way he had felt when he had rejected her pleas to turn back to Starbase One. Cold fingers clamped about his heart, then squeezed slowly until Kirk felt as if he'd start to gasp. He didn't know if this physical reaction to the woman bothered him as much as his mounting anger at McCoy, at Mek Jokkor, at Zarv, at all the others.

"What's wrong with the *Enterprise?*" he demanded, slamming a fist down against the communications console. Uhura looked up, startled. Sulu and Chekov both peered over their shoulders from their posts. Others on the bridge cast sidelong glances at their captain before returning to their duties.

"Captain, the ship is in need of specific repairs, but other than that, nothing is wrong with it."

"Dammit, Spock, don't be so literal. I mean the crew. Why is McCoy arguing with Mek Jokkor? He has no place to. Where'd he get the idea that the Federation is being used by Ammdon?"

"It seems a plausible maneuver on the part of a developing world. Our interests range farther than theirs, and they see the chance for specific gain while we pursue a more general position."

"In other words, you're agreeing with Lor—" Kirk stopped, swallowed, then continued. "You're agreeing with McCoy that Ammdon is playing us for the fool, that the *Enterprise* will be dragged into this war on their side against Jurnamoria."

"It is conceivable, but one must take into account the experience and superior knowledge of the negotiating team sent by the Federation Council. Zarv's record, for all his personal truculence, is impeccable. He is no one's fool—or tool."

"Neither is Lorritson. Or, I suspect, Mek Jokkor."

"Quite correct, Captain."

This soothed some of the emotional storm raging within, but anger remained. "McCoy. Has he spoken with Lorelei recently? Within the past hour or two?"

"Unknown, Captain. Why not ask the doctor?" Spock's focus shifted to a point behind his commander. Kirk turned to see McCoy striding onto the bridge, a grim expression set on his craggy face.

"Jim, I want to protest about that refugee from a succotash."

"Mek Jokkor?"

"Yeah, the plant fellow. He insulted me. Made me angry. I don't like that."

"I'm sure you don't." Kirk started to say he'd listened to the transcript of the argument, then decided to take a different tack. If the doctor knew he'd been spied upon, he'd become totally unreasonable and nothing would be resolved. For whatever reason, Kirk sensed that this entire matter reached far beyond simple disagreement between medical doctor and diplomatic aide.

"He wanted to continue on this snipe hunt, and I think

we ought to turn around and go home. The crew needs rest. The ship is falling apart. As a medical opinion, absolutely official, mind you, it is my recommendation to return to base."

"Your appraisal is noted, Doctor. I've seen the signs of fatigue mounting. I'm not blind. But you must also take into account the dire situation that exists between Ammdon and Jurnamoria."

"Ammdon is using us."

"No doubt Mek Jokkor realizes that possibility. I am certain Zarv and Lorritson do, also. Tell me, Bones, before you and Mek Jokkor got involved in your, uh, discussion, what were you doing?"

"Doing? Nothing. My job. How should I know? I don't keep a minute-by-minute diary."

"Maybe you should. It'd make checking up on certain items easier for me."

"Such as?" demanded the doctor, squaring his shoulders and bracing himself, as if getting ready for a fight.

"I needed to know about Lorelei's condition, for example. She's not quite human. It'd be a shame to allow her to slowly die from trace-element deficiencies in her diet, for instance. She's been through a lot, poor girl."

Kirk felt the tightness around his heart again as he mentioned the woman's name. Something about her was not normal. Certainly his responses to her weren't normal.

"Checked her out completely just before I got into it with that animated rutabaga. She's fine, Jim. Don't worry about her."

"How long did her examination take?" Kirk tried to sound nonchalant about it, yet his tenseness communicated itself to McCoy.

"I'm a doctor," said McCoy, his voice as cold as the vacuum of space. "I don't like your insinuation. Nurse Chapel was in the room the entire examination. And afterward all Lorelei and I did was talk about this damned so-called peace mission."

"I apologize, Bones. I didn't mean to imply you'd done anything unethical."

The doctor shook his head and left the bridge. Kirk sat in his command seat and drummed restless fingers against the armrest. Lorelei had spoken to Bones McCoy minutes before the argument with Mek Jokkor and less than a half hour prior to her meeting with Kirk in his cabin. McCoy had swallowed her beliefs as completely as matter and antimatter interact. And he hadn't realized it.

Kirk rubbed his temples. His head began throbbing with a migraine pain that refused to die down.

"Look at this, Kirk. Just look at it!" Ambassador Zarv shook the flimsy sheet of paper under the captain's nose. "It is the latest subspace radio communiqué from Starbase One. They report heightened tensions between Ammdon and Jurnamoria. To make it all the worse, the Romulans are moving heavy cruisers to the demarcation line. They will invade soon, and all because you are a fool!"

The piglike diplomat snorted and began pawing at the hard deck plate. His pudgy hands shook uncontrollably and his eyes widened in anger until the whites showed entirely around his irises. Kirk thought the Tellarite was on the point of losing control.

"Ambassador Zarv, the message is important. I grant that, but I also have to take into consideration the condition of my ship. To increase speed now is out of the question."

"Then peace will be out of the question. Kirk," said the Tellarite diplomat in a fierce voice, "you will be responsible for plunging the entire Orion Arm into war for the next hundred years. The Federation might never recover our position because you refused to squeeze a little tighter on the engines and get my team there in time!"

James Kirk fought down his own anger. Why wouldn't Zarv listen? The Tellarite's fanaticism concerning the Romulans was understandable, after what Donald Lorritson had told him. Zarv's entire family had been killed by the Romulans in a brief incursion years before. His hatred for them and all they stood for transcended mere duty; it took on personal overtones. But the diplomat refused to consider anything not directly bearing on his mission.

"Which would you prefer, Ambassador?" spoke up Spock. "To possibly arrive sooner, due to increased speed, and take the chance of the engines being destroyed and thereby *never* arriving, or to maintain current speed and be assured of arrival, albeit later than you desire?"

"What is this, a guessing game? You know my preference. Speed *and* arrival. Pash!" The Tellarite crammed the subspace message into his jacket pocket and stormed off, leaving Donald Lorritson behind. Lorritson straightened and tugged slightly at the tails of his impeccable high-dinner jacket.

"The ambassador is upset due to the nature of the message, Captain," Lorritson began.

"I appreciate that, but I want you to consider that one of my engineering chiefs is in sick bay because of a stabilizer-circuit malfunction. It wasn't a fatal accident, but it points up the dangers involved in pushing crew and ships beyond their limit."

The relief Kirk experienced at having said his piece washed over him. There was scant need to remain silent on either his feelings or the actual condition of the *Enterprise*. But the sensation faded quickly and Kirk once more experienced the nightmare fantasy of being trapped in the jaws of a nutcracker. On the one hand he fought the growing need to abandon the mission and return to starbase—as Lorelei desired—and on the other there was Zarv and his insistence on not only continuing with the mission but throwing caution to the winds and rocketing forward at emergency speeds.

Donald Lorritson studied him for a moment, then quietly said, "It is not easy being the captain of a starship. It isn't easy, either, being responsible for the destinies of two planets on the brink of war—with the added danger of Romulan incursion."

"We understand one another, Mr. Lorritson. I only wish your ambassador would make the effort to do likewise."

"He knows, sir. The Tellarite makeup is not ideal for quiet discussion or," he said, turning toward Spock, "logical debate. In certain situations, such as this one, such a personality makes Zarv ideal."

"It is difficult to believe."

Lorritson smiled wanly. "You haven't met the Ammdons or the Jurnamorians."

"I have encountered the Romulans, and that alone makes me agree to continue pushing both my ship and personnel to the limit."

"Thank you, Captain. Now I must join Zarv and Mek Jokkor. We are analyzing potential approaches to the problem facing us."

"The computer is yours."

Lorritson nodded curtly, then left. Kirk focused his eyes on the forward viewscreen. Warp factor one caused the stars to creep by, as if they had been dipped in some sort of cosmic glue. His only hope for getting out of the nutcracker's jaws was to deliver the diplomatic team as swiftly as possible.

But Lorelei's words were so beguiling. . . .

* * *

"So the Scotsman smooths his kilt after lookin' at the blue ribbon and says, 'Well, me wee bairn, I don't know where ye been or what ye been doin', but ye took first prize!'" Heather McConel finished the joke just as Kirk walked into the engineering design office. The redheaded chief sucked in her breath and turned to stare straight ahead at a blank bulkhead. Kirk pretended he hadn't heard the punch line at all.

Montgomery Scott noted the sudden change in his chief's demeanor and spun in the swivel seat to face the door. When he saw his captain, his face flushed.

"As you were," snapped Kirk. "Scotty, a word with you. Outside."

"Aye, sair." Scotty shot a venomous look at McConel, then followed Kirk out into the corridor. "What ye heard isn't as it seems, Captain."

"That joke? Scotty, it's so old it creaks. And why should I care if my crew tells jokes?"

"Ye don't mind, then?"

"I have more pressing matters to worry about. Such as the engines. What's their status?"

"Captain, they're nae so good." Scotty always told him that. Kirk dismissed it with a wave of his hand, demanding to know the precise condition of the warp engines. "This time I mean it, sair. I kenna little else to do to help the poor things."

"Can you get me warp three for any length of time?"

"Impossible," the dour Scotsman declared with conviction. "Even at warp two, it'd be chancy. Unless . . ."

"Yes?"

"Well, Captain, there's a chance—a long one—that Chief McConel and I can do a wee bit of tinkerin'. Just a chance, mind you."

"How much? How fast, Scotty? What can I expect? When?"

Scotty shook his head before replying. "I dinna want to raise your hopes like this. It might be nothin'."

"Scotty," said Kirk, slapping the engineer on the back, "knowing you, it'll be something. What are you thinking about?"

"The stabilizer for the exciter circuit is what's limitin' us. With constant vigilance, we might be able to hold things together at warp three. But not one wee bit more!"

"Do it, Scotty, and I'll see that Admiral McKenna personally gives you a commendation."

"Keep the commendation, sair. Just let me rebuild the engines in peace once we return to starbase."

"Done. You and Chief McConel get to work. I'll check back in an hour." Kirk watched Scotty herd his red-haired chief out of the design room and down the corridor toward the engine room. All the way they hotly debated Scotty's newest scheme. They vanished around a bend in the corridor, and Kirk strode off in the opposite direction. He had to check in with Spock to make certain everything else in the *Enterprise* functioned to perfection.

"Heather," called out Montgomery Scott, "increase power level by ten paircent, then cut back when I tell you." He balanced precariously atop a jury-rigged ladder to reach part of the stabilizer circuit not meant for casual inspection. A long-armed quantum wrench vanished through the bulkhead access port and into the guts of the exciter stabilizer.

Nothing happened. His keen eyes watched the meter movement, and the readout never wavered from its norm. Scotty twisted about and peered down at the engineering control panel where Heather McConel stood, hands on dials.

"What's wrong?" he called. "There's nae even a wee movement in the readin'."

Still nothing. Scotty cursed under his breath, braced the wrench so he wouldn't have to reposition it later, then retraced his way down the makeshift ladder built from boxes and scrap aluminum tubing. He dropped to the deck and turned to find why his chief hadn't responded. His Scottish anger rose when he saw Heather McConel talking with Lorelei, hands gesticulating in a manner that showed his redheaded chief was totally absorbed in the conversation.

"Chief McConel," he said loudly, "why are you nae tendin' to duty like I ordered?"

"Huh? Oh, Scotty, I want ye to listen to what the lass has to say. I find it a mite perplexing, but maybe you can make heads or tails out of it."

He stalked over, his anger mounting at the delay. He'd been ordered by his captain to get the most possible from the engines. They strained and whined in a most unbecoming manner. Considerable retuning would be required before the *Enterprise* mounted even a steady warp-two speed, much less the warp three that Kirk desired. This mousy-haired alien only distracted him and his technicians from the work at hand. Scotty didn't like it. He didn't like it at all, and it startled him that Heather put up with the interruption.

"What is it?" He stood, hands balled on hips.

"Commander Scott," Lorelei said in a low, coaxing voice, "I do so hate to disturb you, but I wanted to see how an expert engineer worked. You keep the engines in such fine form."

Her words took some of the heat from his anger. Still . . .

"Lass, that's a fine thing you're sayin' about me and the engines, but we do have work to do."

"Work that will destroy the entire ship."

"What?"

"This is what I wanted ye to hear, Scotty," spoke up Heather. "Lorelei has some interesting things to say. They make sense."

"I canna take the time to listen to wild stories." Scotty's resolve faded as he looked at Lorelei. She appeared no lovelier to him than she had before; Heather was more like a fine lass ought to be. But Lorelei's aspect altered subtly in his mind. She seemed more commanding, more competent, more knowledgeable. The small woman radiated an air of *competence*. Scotty appreciated that.

The least he could do was afford her a few seconds.

"What is it ye have to say?"

Scotty and Heather found themselves listening enraptured as the woman began speaking. Her voice carried conviction, appeal, touched all the right spots in her listeners' psyches. In spite of himself, Scotty found he agreed more and more. The few times he began to protest, Lorelei countered his arguments in such a fashion he found himself lost in a maelstrom of logic and evidence. It became easier to believe her than to disbelieve.

Lorelei left the two behind, quietly talking over all she'd said. No hint of accomplishment showed on the petite woman's features. Only sadness. Extreme sadness.

"Scotty!" called out James Kirk. "How's it going? Scotty?" Kirk looked around the engineering deck. The control panels were deserted and no human stirred. He heard quiet electronic humming as relays shunted immense amounts of power back and forth from the engines through the stabilizer circuits controlling the magnetic bottles holding in the hellfire of the matter-antimatter reaction. But no human sounds.

"Scotty? McConel?" Irritation was slowly displaced by

nagging fear. Something was amiss. Scotty didn't abandon his post. Especially not when the adjustments needed to the engines were critical. Commander Scott would live, eat, sleep and breathe engines until they performed to fullest capacity. Going off and taking his entire staff with him ran counter to all the man believed in.

Kirk went to the intercom and punched the button. "Bridge? Get me Spock."

A muted voice on the other end mumbled, to be replaced by the Vulcan's crisp acknowledgment.

"Spock, do you know where Mr. Scott is? I can't seem to locate him."

"He is not at his post?"

"Neither is Heather McConel."

"Peculiar. One moment, Captain." Kirk impatiently shifted his weight from one foot to the other as he waited for his science officer to interrogate the ship's computer. In less than ten seconds Spock's voice echoed from the speaker. "I find no life-form readings on engineering deck other than yours. However, there are many unusual readings coming from the engineering design laboratory. Is it possible Mr. Scott is there conducting appropriate experiments?"

"Possible, Spock, but I wonder. Check out the engines. What are the power levels?"

"Warp factor one, sir, but there is some indication that power levels are deteriorating at a rate that will leave us adrift in less than forty hours."

"You mean the engines are being throttled back?"

"Precisely, Captain."

Kirk slammed his fist into the intercom button and broke the connection. He stormed from the engineering deck to the design lab. Scotty and Heather sat at the large table in the center of the room, a dozen others from the engineering staff arrayed around them like apostles at the Last Supper.

"What's the meaning of cutting back on the power, Scotty? After I ordered increased speed?"

The expression on Scott's face puzzled Kirk. His engineer might be angry or contrite or happy, but seldom had he seen him confused. The man almost stuttered, his confusion was so great.

"Captain, we been discussin' the engines. 'Tis not a good situation we have developin'."

"The magnetic bottles?" Kirk asked anxiously. The thought of those magnetic shields rupturing and letting out the prodigious power of the matter-antimatter reaction made him pause. The *Enterprise* wouldn't explode—it'd vanish as surely as if they'd been instantaneously thrust into the core of a sun.

"They are holding fine, Captain Kirk," said Heather McConel. "It's that we kenna this mission."

"You're questioning the purpose of our going to Ammdon?" Kirk stood stock-still. Shock shattered his composure. McConel was the last he'd expected to ever question a command decision.

"Aye, Captain, Heather speaks for all of us."

"Scotty?" The shock turned him cold all over.

"Captain, the *Enterprise* will be destroyed if we continue on. There's got to be an end to this suicide mission. I ordered the engines to be cycled down."

"Spock is correcting that," said Kirk, his resolve returning. "What you're doing is disobeying a direct order, Scotty. You realize what that can mean?"

"Aye, court-martial. But it's nae better bein' atoms scattered amongst the stars."

"Mr. Scott, you will return to your post. You and Chief

McConel will put as much power to the engines, you will develop as much speed, as possible, you will do your duty. Those are direct orders. Do you understand me?"

"Aye, Captain, but—"

"Mister Scott, there are no 'buts' in this matter. Do your duty, sir!"

James Kirk turned and stalked out, not wanting to see what reaction his orders had. He almost feared open disobedience. And Scotty was the last one of the crew he'd ever want to court-martial for failure to perform his duty.

"What's happening? Why's this damned Ammdon-Jurnamoria mess affecting my crew?" But, deep down, Kirk knew the answer. Something buried in his psyche prevented him from squarely facing it.

"I can't believe it, Spock. They're not at their posts. It's as if they don't care about their work." Kirk looked around the bridge and saw several tight clusters of officers, ignoring their duty stations and quietly talking among themselves.

"Distraction is a human condition I have studied but do not fully understand. I fail to comprehend how anyone can lose concentration while engaged on a project."

"Get them back to their stations." Kirk watched as Spock slowly orbited the bridge and chased the crew back to work. As the Vulcan science officer had noted, the crew did not openly disobey. That was a nightmare of Kirk's that had little basis in reality. Even after they had returned to their posts, however, they worked in a desultory fashion, obviously engrossed in—what?

"Do you wish to see my report on ship's status?"

"Hmm? Oh, yes, Spock." Kirk bent over the computer console and watched the visual display rather than allowing Spock to turn it to verbal. He wanted as few on the bridge as possible to share the report. After a few lines, Kirk was glad he'd decided on such secrecy. The status of most ship's systems was far from optimal.

"Explain, Spock. Why is everything falling apart? It's not simply because we didn't get rebuilt while in dry dock. Systems like life support were in excellent condition."

"They are no longer. Neglect, Captain. Inattention to detail. It seems that the crew is more inclined to gather and talk in a clandestine fashion."

"The canceled shore leave. That must be it. Post a bulletin, Spock, informing all crew members that they'll receive an extra two weeks' leave when we return to starbase."

"Captain, this inattention runs more sinister than tiredness or disappointment over lack of leave."

"Explain, Spock." Kirk didn't like the ominous implications of his science officer's statement.

"I fear that open disobedience will turn to mutiny."

Kirk snorted in disgust at the idea. "Spock, be realistic. My crew will not mutiny. Why should they? The *Enterprise* is the finest ship in Starfleet. I work them hard, but the rewards are great. Advancement is better on board, training is better, just about everything is better."

"The systems are malfunctioning because of neglect, Captain. The crew is not following standing orders concerning maintenance, and many are agitating for a union."

"What do you mean by a 'union'? I don't understand."

"It is a term employed during the twentieth and twenty-first centuries on Earth. A group of workers with mutual concerns and complaints elects one of their number to address the grievances with those in a position of power and able to alter the conditions."

"Mr. Spock, this is *not* a democracy. We are a ship responsible to Starfleet. Voting on every decision is not only impractical, it is impossible and highly dangerous. We must rely on experts in various fields. While I am knowledgeable about engines, I cannot repair them like Scotty can. Likewise, my training and experience are in command. I am ordered to get the negotiating team to Ammdon by my superiors and must do it to the best of my ability. Those orders are not open to veto by a vote of the crew."

"You do not have to explain, Captain. I merely provided a datum requested."

"Don't get touchy on me now, Spock. I've just never even heard of such . . ." Words failed him as he looked around his bridge. Sulu and Chekov argued in voices too low to be overheard. Uhura and the on-duty bridge engineering officer carried on a similar discussion. "What's going on?" Kirk ended up saying, feeling helpless.

"It is my belief," said Spock in his clipped tones, "that the crew of the *Enterprise* is preparing to mutiny."

# Chapter Four

*Captain's Log,* Stardate 4822.9

I have tolerated the crew's growing inattention to duty long enough. While the strain of maintaining a starship is considerable, the *Enterprise* crew is one of the best in Starfleet Command. It is *the* best. Spock and I must monitor constantly all vital systems to prevent disaster. It is inconceivable to me that postponed shore leave is the root cause of this dereliction of duty, but it is the only plausible reason. I will assemble my section heads and put a stop to this at once. Otherwise, we will arrive in the Ammdon-Jurnamoria system in a condition little better than a decrepit garbage scow.

James Kirk sat in his quarters, ears straining to pick up the bootheels clicking in the corridor just beyond his door.

Increased traffic indicated that his orders were being followed—at least for the moment. He'd come down hard on several of the junior officers when he'd discovered them in the wardroom talking rather than at their duty stations. While the ripples from his discipline would soon die out to nothing, he hoped that the momentum gathered from once again performing their tasks adequately would continue.

But he didn't kid himself too much on this score.

Spock had once again warned him of the possibility of mutiny. Whether he refused to believe such dire things of the *Enterprise* crew or whether his own ego got tangled up in it and he couldn't consider it happening to him, he discounted such as fantasy.

"Fantasy," he muttered to himself, eyes focused on the far side of his quarters. His attention slowly pulled in closer to the computer readout screen. The report silently marching across the face unnerved him. He'd punched in a request to the library computer for all instances of mutiny aboard Starfleet vessels.

There had been only a handful in Starfleet's history, but those five mutinies chilled Kirk to the bone. The reports were, of necessity, incomplete and biased, but he managed to infer much that had never reached the computer data banks. The crews mutinying had all been pushed beyond the limits of human endurance, more demanded of them than might be expected. Aboard the USS *Farallones* the captain had been a martinet in addition to ordering his crew into a potentially hazardous condition in the demilitarized zone between the Romulan Empire and the Federation. The captain, a career officer named MacCallum, had been killed, but the ringleaders of the mutiny had been sent to a penal colony for life, no rehabilitation considered possible. What galled Kirk the most was that the mutineers had been right and MacCallum wrong—his actions might have triggered war between the Romulans and the Federation.

Still, the *Farallones* crew had been given orders and they had willfully disobeyed.

"Am I leading the *Enterprise* into a war?" he asked aloud. "I have my orders. The diplomatic team is the finest the Federation can send. They intend to prevent a war, not start one. There's no reason for the crew to show such antipathy to the mission."

His words failed to comfort him or convince him of the rightness of his position. Kirk glanced at the chronometer and saw that the time had arrived. He rose, smoothed his tunic and left his quarters, heading for the wardroom.

"As you were," he said automatically as the door whispered shut behind him. Usually his officers snapped to attention when he entered the room. This time many of them were too busy muttering among themselves to even notice his presence. He ignored their oversight of protocol.

"Captain, all section heads are present or accounted for." Spock's eyes darted about the large table at several vacant chairs. Kirk wanted to inquire as to those missing but didn't. Spock had said they were accounted for. That had to be good enough. For the moment.

"Ladies and gentlemen, there is a growing misapprehension among crew members as to who exactly is in command of the *Enterprise*." He paused a few seconds to make certain he had their undivided attention. He did. "I am in command of this vessel. Do I make myself clear on this point?"

"Uh, sir, isn't that apparent?" asked Lieutenant Patten, the head of security. "You're the captain, after all."

"That seems to have been overlooked recently, Lieutenant. I'm referring to the shoddiness of performance on the parts of *all* the crew. I'm not singling out any individual section. I don't have to—all are equally guilty of what I consider one of the worst possible infractions of Starfleet discipline."

"That's unfair, sir," spoke up Commander Buchanan. She rose and leaned forward on the palms of her hands in an unconscious duplication of the pose Kirk had struck. "We've about reached the end of our endurance. Now that you're leading us into a battle zone—"

"Who told you that, Commander? Who?" When the woman didn't answer, Kirk straightened and peered from one face to the next. What he saw didn't please him in the least. There was outright skepticism about the mission of the *Enterprise*. "I want to inform you all—officially—that we are not going to the Ammdon star system to foment war. Rather, our purpose is as it has always been: we are promoting peace among all intelligent races."

Someone at the table gave a derisive snort.

"The diplomatic team aboard the *Enterprise* is specially chosen for their skill in such negotiations. There will be no war. If we arrive in the Ammdon-Jurnamoria system in time to prevent it."

"The Romulans are already there," one of the officers said. "We'll have to fight it out with them. If we even try, they'll blow us into cosmic dust. The ship's not up to combat."

"Mister," Kirk answered coldly, "the ship will not be entering combat. The Romulans do not occupy the Ammdon system and will not have the opportunity if the Federation's diplomatic mission is successful. It will fail—if you do not shape up those in your sections. You are Starfleet officers. You are expected to obey commands and to promote and protect the peace, in all sectors of the galaxy."

"Fine words, Captain, but that's not the way it is," said Commander Buchanan. "When we show up, that'll be Ammdon's signal to launch the war. It'll look as if we're supporting them. That will force Jurnamoria into an alliance with the Romulans, and war will be declared just a few minutes after the treaty is drafted."

"You are too certain about this. All of you. And the words come out sounding the same, as if it isn't your own idea. Dr. McCoy." Kirk faced his friend, who shook his head and glowered at the exchange that had just occurred.

"Yes, Captain?"

"You were the first to bring this interesting theory to my attention. Where did you get the idea that we would precipitate war rather than prevent it?"

"Why, it's my own conclusion. Hell, Jim, it's as plain as horns on a bull."

Kirk cut him off. "I also heard a similar argument from the alien we discovered in the wreck. Did Lorelei speak to you about this situation before you came to me?"

"Well, she might have. But what's that got to do—"

"And you others. Think about it. Did Lorelei sway your thinking?" Kirk fought the tightness in his throat that came when even mentioning the alien woman. So potent a hold prevented him from being fully rational when he spoke of her, yet he had to. The fate of their mission depended on getting his officers straightened out. The fate of the *Enterprise* also depended on it. That, as much as anything else, kept him talking, kept their attention to the matter at hand, kept him from succumbing to the woman's mysterious power.

"I spoke with her," said Lieutenant Patten. "But it wasn't about Ammdon. We just . . . talked. I like her." A half grin crossed the man's face, giving him a slightly comical expression. No one laughed. Most of them had similar smiles as they thought about Lorelei.

"Liking her has nothing to do with whether or not we carry out our orders from Starfleet Command."

"Begging your pardon, sir, but I believe that might have a decided bearing on it." Spock raised one slender finger and placed it alongside his cheek. The light shining from the computer screen gave him a demonic appearance, the flickering turning his sallow skin a pale blue and highlighting the arched eyebrows.

"Go on, Mr. Spock. I'm interested in your theories."

"Not a theory but rather a conjecture. We know nothing of Lorelei's home planet, this Hyla. We know little of her culture except what she has revealed. From her title Speaker, we must infer that she has some ability in that regard."

"Brilliant," muttered McCoy. "And for this I left my surgery?"

Kirk ignored the almost-whispered comment and Spock only cast a sidelong glance at the doctor before continuing. "She is a first-rate orator capable of swaying those who listen to her. Her pacifistic views were expressed soon after we rescued her. It is plausible that she promulgates this philosophy so effectively that it is beginning to affect the crew's performance."

"Isn't that a bit farfetched?" Kirk leaned back in his chair and stared at his science officer. "You're attributing superhuman powers to her."

"Not superhuman, Captain, but definitely alien powers. Dr. McCoy will testify that she survived in a spacecraft bathed with deadly radiations far longer than any human or Vulcan could have endured. Her life-form readings are different in ways that the doctor is unable to explain."

"She lives off our atmosphere and our food well enough,"

protested McCoy. "You're making her out to be some sideshow freak. Leastways, she doesn't have pointed ears."

"Bones, quiet." Kirk shot the doctor a second look that stifled all further response. "Spock, do you have any proof for these allegations? If what you're saying is true, Lorelei is quite dangerous."

"Not physically dangerous, sir. But she is committed to a philosophy at odds with the course we follow."

"We're trying to maintain peace, dammit. Why is everyone claiming the reverse?"

"Anger will gain you nothing and clouds your logical processes." Kirk started to retort, then saw that Spock was right. He gestured for the Vulcan to continue. Spock inclined his head slightly and explained his position. "She has adequate reason to believe we say one thing and will do another. She is as much a stranger to our ways as we are to hers. Her logic tells her that she is right; to be true to her beliefs she uses this . . . talent . . . of hers to alter opinion among the crew."

"That is ascribing powers to her I don't believe she has, Mr. Spock." Captain Kirk studied the set faces of his officers and came to a conclusion. Something had to be done, and it wouldn't happen here. "I am authorizing a shipwide debate over this matter between Lorelei and Ambassador Zarv. I have full confidence that the ambassador will adequately put all fears to rest as to the purpose of our mission. See to the arrangements, Mr. Spock."

The only response he received was a slight facial twitch from his science officer. That upset Kirk more than if Spock had openly opposed him. He quickly stood and left the room.

He'd done the right thing. He was sure of it.

* * *

"This is ill advised, Captain. I wish you had discussed it with me prior to announcing the debate to the other officers."

"Spock, you lack faith."

"Sir, I do not lack confidence in my abilities, only in those demonstrated throughout the crew. However, this is not a satisfactory course to follow given the potentially mutinous feelings aboard ship."

"There will be no further talk of mutiny," snapped Kirk. "It's something that happens if you speak of it too often."

"That is superstition and illogical in the extreme. I offer facts."

Before Kirk replied, a familiar snorting noise boomed down the hall and burst into the room where technicians had set up the video link required to carry the debate to all sections of the ship.

"Kirk," bellowed Ambassador Zarv, "why am I supposed to debate with, of all things, that emaciated wisp of a child? What do you use for brains besides space dust?"

"Ambassador, the situation aboard ship is unique in my experience. I felt that an informal discussion of our policies, of our peace mission, of what the Federation hopes to accomplish by sending one of its top negotiators to Ammdon, would be helpful. Lorelei cannot possibly defend any contrary position, can she?"

"Of course not."

Behind the Tellarite ambassador, Donald Lorritson smiled at Kirk's maneuverings. The man obviously appreciated how the captain had diplomatically herded Zarv into carrying through with the debate.

"Excellent. Lorelei will be here in a moment and we can begin."

Zarv snorted, then said, "Perhaps this won't be a waste

of time, Lorritson. I can try out some of the reasonings we developed and see the reaction. The crew of a starship is likely to respond as those Orion Arm yokels will."

"A fine chance to sharpen your histrionic skills," agreed Lorritson.

Mek Jokkor slid into the room and stood under one of the floodlights, basking in it as only a plant can appreciate light. Kirk imagined he saw the photosynthesis strengthening arms and legs.

Spock took his captain's arm and pulled him to one side, saying in a low voice, "Jim, there is still time to stop this ill-conceived meeting. If Lorelei is as I believe, then she will have the—"

"Lorelei!" called out Kirk, pulling away from Spock. The small, brown-haired woman glided into the room as if she rolled on wheels rather than walking on feet. Every move was graceful and coordinated. "You decided to participate in the discussion. I'm glad." He grinned when he saw her expression. She did not appear the least bit happy.

"Captain, what I do does not please me, but for peace I do what I must."

"We all do what we can—in the name of galactic peace."

"Tell me about this." She gestured toward the tri-vid cameras. "We do not have such things on Hyla."

"Your three-dimensional image will be carried throughout the ship. All the wardrooms are equipped with receivers, and we installed them in several other meeting rooms."

"My image will appear. As will my voice?"

"Of course. It wouldn't do to show only your lovely form."

"Captain, you are too good to me." Kirk felt a warmth creeping inside him. She wasn't even pretty, he finally decided, but attractive. Definitely attractive, and that encompassed intellect, grace, dignity, so many items other than the elusive symmetrical quality known as beauty. A beauty of the soul, he decided, rather than merely physical.

"Let's be done with this," bellowed Zarv. "I still have much preparation to do before arrival in the Ammdon system, and Kirk insists on dawdling at virtually sublight speeds."

"Begin when you like," ordered Kirk. "Ambassador, do you wish to speak first?"

"Very well."

The Tellarite's manner changed as if he had dropped a completely new blanketing personality over himself. The truculence vanished the instant the indicator light glowed on the holographic camera. Zarv spoke decisively, concisely and with a conviction that made Kirk turn toward Spock and smile, as if telling his science officer that logic didn't always work, that gut-level instinct and trust in others sometimes paid off handsomely.

Spock sidled up to his captain and said in a voice too low to be picked up by the microphones, "This is a mistake. Everyone on board is listening. You must not allow Lorelei to speak."

"You worry too much. Listen to Zarv. That's why he's an ambassador. The man's tongue caresses the words. He's persuasive. You can even get over the fact that he looks like a pig."

"His appearance is not in question, Captain."

Kirk put an index finger over his lips to signal silence. Spock subsided, obviously uneasy. Kirk wanted nothing more than to listen to Zarv's arguments for the Ammdon mission. They would put to rest all the critics aboard the *Enterprise*. At the end of a ten-minute presentation, Zarv finished, saying, "Thank you for allowing me the opportunity to present the truth in this matter." He sat down, and Lorelei moved into the focus of the cameras.

"See how ineffectual she looks?" Kirk said. "Compare her delivery techniques with those Zarv used. The Tellarite is a master diplomat. A master."

Kirk leaned back and waited for Lorelei to begin. She'd not have a chance if he polled the crew as to their opinions afterward. Zarv was a professional, and she was hardly more than a girl.

The Speaker of Hyla began.

And James Kirk felt the surging power of her words, the deft precision, the urgency and the emotion. She drew him out, pushed him to the heights of ecstasy, drew tears from his eyes and then turned him inside out—and all with her words. For the first time he understood what Ammdon intended to do. The *Enterprise* was a pawn, of that she convinced him. The Romulan incursion would become a fact if the *Enterprise* entered the Ammdon system; Jurnamoria had no choice but to align itself with the Empire.

"Captain, stop this now," urged Spock. "You are affected. Even I sense the potency of her words. What they are doing to the crew is incalculable."

"But she's right, Spock. How could we have been so misled? Listen! She's showing us the truth." Kirk leaned forward, as if this might get him even better understanding of the deadly situation. He ignored Zarv's protests from the side. Donald Lorritson spoke rapidly to his superior, and they went into immediate conference. Mek Jokkor stood silently at one side, enjoying the radiance from the lamps more than anything else.

And James T. Kirk listened, really *listened* for the first time.

"She's right, Spock. We must—"

The ship shuddered as if a giant fist had seized it and had begun shaking. Seconds later the alarms went off, deafening everyone in the room. Lights flickered and emergency beams cut in.

Kirk rocketed to his feet and hit the intercom button. "Scotty, report. What the hell's happened?"

"Sair," came the engineer's quavering voice. "We lost the magnetic bottle on the port side. I've had to shut down the power. Otherwise, we'd have been destroyed. Sair, the *Enterprise* is in mortal danger of blowin' up!"

# Chapter Five

*Captain's Log,* Supplemental:

> The extent of the damage to the *Enterprise* is as yet unknown. I fear that it will be both extensive and potentially dangerous for all on board. With the warp engines down, both our transporter and subspace radio capacity are drastically limited, if not destroyed. While there are other methods for alerting Starbase One of our plight, I'd prefer to remain under power and attempt completion of our mission. This might not be possible. If it is not, these will be the first orders I have been unable to obey. The possibility of failure is not one I easily accept.

"You'll require a radiation suit before entering, Captain," said Spock, halting James Kirk just outside the doorway leading into the engineering section. Red lights flashed balefully and the shrill whine of a distant warning siren continued to assault his hearing. "The entire area around the warp engines is flooded with hard gamma and x-rays from the exposed antimatter."

"Get me a suit," he ordered one of the passing crewmen. The man appeared stunned but obeyed, moving as if all volition had been erased from him. Kirk quickly climbed into the bulky protective garment provided. By the time he pushed the button opening the door leading into the radiation-drenched area, Spock had donned a similar suit. Together they slipped into the engine room.

Kirk's first impression was that he'd been the victim of a gigantic hoax. Everything appeared normal—until he saw Scotty's crew frantically working at the control boards. They were decked out in radiation-resistant suits, and many taxed the powers of their suits' air-conditioning units; faceplates fogged over from excess sweat. If that weren't evidence enough, one look at the radiation counters mounted throughout the section convinced Kirk all was not normal.

The digital readings mounted higher than any he'd ever seen outside experimental-station laboratories.

"The radiation level is only a few orders of magnitude less than that attained in the center of the working matter-antimatter module," said Spock. "We would die instantly without our suits."

"Where's Scotty? I want to speak with him." Kirk and Spock skirted the struggling technicians and found Montgomery Scott and Heather McConel ripping open the guts of a panel and plunging into the maze of integrated and cubic circuitry with an abandon that startled Kirk. Scotty usually treated equipment with almost religious reverence. Now the ship's master engineer tore loose fittings and discarded electronic parts as if they were so much junk.

"The radiation has destroyed the functional capabilities," explained Spock. "Mr. Scott is trying to reach the auxiliary bypass cutoff circuits. It is necessary to totally curtail power in both engines until damage can be assessed."

"'Tis true, Captain," said Chief McConel, momentarily looking up from her demolition activity in the complex electronic maze. "Commander Scott's done all he could, but it does nae look so good."

"Heather, your hands are smaller. Get to it." Scotty backed away and let his assistant drop into the space he'd occupied. For the first time he saw Kirk and Spock. The man shook his head. "We might nae make it, Captain. 'Tis that bad."

"Report."

In a voice laced with infinite tiredness Scotty said, "The magnetic bottles did nae rupture as I'd feared, but spots in the bottle walls thinned to the point where enough radiation escaped into this compartment to fuse circuits. That triggered all the alarms. We're workin' to contain the radiation leakage and completely shut down the matter-antimatter reaction."

"If you shut it down, it'll require a starbase dry dock to restart!" protested Kirk. "We're light-years from a starbase with adequate facilities. That'll mean we'll be stranded without faster-than-light drive capability."

"If we dinna shut down, we'll go *poof!*" Scotty gestured, indicating how the *Enterprise* would simply vanish in one dazzling actinic flare. "But I kenna if the engines can be restarted. Possibly."

"Are you referring to the Rotsler technique?" asked Spock. "It is only a theoretical procedure and has never been attempted empirically during actual emergency conditions in space."

"What is this, this Rotsler technique?" demanded Kirk.

"If Scotty shuts down the warp engines, are you saying we can restart them after repairs are made?"

"Possibly, though it requires materiel we do not have aboard ship. A considerable amount of shielding is necessary, simply for repairs. To approximate restart using the aforementioned method requires even more radiation blanketing. The engines must be totally encased in shielding, trapping all—or most—radiation until the environment heats to ignition point. It is not a cold-start procedure, but rather one characterized as warm start."

"What kind of shielding? All we have is a few centimeters of lead shielding and some force-screen equipment."

"Totally inadequate," declared Spock.

"Aye, Captain, the Vulcan's right. The kinda shieldin' we're requirin' is a dozen meters of mercury or lead. Nothin' less than this will do for us."

"A dozen meters?" Kirk turned and looked back toward the doorway. He'd only come ten paces. Scotty required more than that distance of lead or mercury in thickness—and the engines were each a hundred meters long.

"That's impossible."

"Aye, I'm afraid so," said the Scotsman, his expression grim.

Kirk refused to consider the chance that they'd all be marooned in space, light-years away from home. What no one mentioned, although each knew it, was that their subspace radio required warp power to operate. With warp-engine power off, their communications capabilities had been diminished severely. If a message packet were to be sent, it'd have to be soon. No matter what happened, they were going to be adrift for many months before aid reached them, even for simple abandonment and scuttling of the ship.

"I will not abandon my vessel," Kirk said forcefully. "And I refuse to believe that our mission cannot be carried out."

Those nearby turned and looked skeptically at him.

"Mr. Scott, continue your work. Do what you can; then report in full. Mr. Spock, begin a detailed analysis of what you'd need to perform this Rotsler technique. And have Sulu and Uhura begin a comprehensive scan of nearby space. We might have overlooked something. This area is not well charted, for all the activity back and forth between the Federation and the Orion Arm."

"Aye, aye, Captain," said Spock. The Vulcan turned and left, his stride firm and unhindered by the bulky radiation suit. Scotty had already returned to his heartbreaking labors. Kirk was left in a sea of misery, staring at the seemingly unharmed engine room. Yet he knew full well that his ship was crippled—perhaps permanently—and that only his crew's expertise prevented them all from being superheated atoms expanding throughout all of space.

He returned to the bridge, worrying as he went.

"Final check of the circuits, sir. Do you wish to confirm?" Spock peered into his computer screen as the steady march of numbers informed him of ship's status.

"Proceed, Mr. Spock." Kirk leaned back in his command seat. Never had it felt harder and more uncomfortable to him. The *Enterprise* had become little more than a derelict vessel helplessly drifting. Scotty had fully shut down the matter-antimatter engines, requiring them to run on only ten percent power, all supplied by emergency battery. This maintained life-support systems and little else until the impulse-power engines were brought to full operating capacity.

"Power coming up," cried Chekov. "Impulse engines to

half, to three-quarters, impulse engines to full power. Sir, do you want me to switch over internal systems now?"

"Do so, Mr. Chekov. I want life support brought up to at least fifty percent norm. Shut down any equipment not performing an essential function. Mr. Spock, prepare a message packet for starbase. I want full computer records of all that's happened included."

"Sir, that does not appear to be possible."

"What do you mean?" The message packet was a self-contained missile with inertial guidance locked on to the nearest starbase. In case of communication blackout, extreme damage as they'd just experienced or the need to send back small material items, the message packet was the preferred method of transport.

"Each of our five packets experienced damage."

"That's impossible, Spock. Those are shielded, protected, damn near coddled. What caused the damage?"

Spock looked up, a slight downward set to his lips. "I can hazard only a guess at this point, Captain. It appears to be an act of sabotage."

Kirk slumped into his seat, pondering the possibilities. Spock never guessed, even if he said so. Hundreds—millions—of tiny bits of evidence went into his evaluation. Perhaps it would never stand up in a court, but Kirk had to believe it was indeed sabotage if Spock "guessed" that it was. He flirted with the idea that it had been Lorelei, but something made him mentally shy away from outright accusation. Others had been affected by her plea that the *Enterprise*'s presence in the Ammdon system would cause a war. The shutdown of the ship's engines presented a perfect reason for not continuing their mission. Anyone listening to Lorelei after Ambassador Zarv had finished might be responsible for the message-packet destruction.

This assured that considerable time would elapse before the Federation sent another diplomatic mission.

Kirk didn't want to even consider the possibility that the warp engines had also been sabotaged.

"Can the message packets be repaired?"

"Impossible. The destruction occurred in the warp-drive mechanisms. They are incapable of attaining light speed, just as the *Enterprise* itself is."

"Dammit, Spock, give me some good news. We're stranded in the middle of nowhere with only impulse power, we can't contact Starbase One, we can't finish our mission, there's no way of repairing the warp engines without shielding we don't have—isn't there any good news?"

"Uh, Captain, I'm picking up something." Sulu twiddled with dials and stroked his fingers over his computer console to bring a wavering picture to the forward viewscreen.

"What is it, Mr. Sulu?"

"It might be a planetary system. Faint star. G class. Obscured by a dust cloud."

"Computing from Mr. Sulu's data," spoke up Spock. "Yes, Captain. You desired good news. This might be it. The system Mr. Sulu has found possesses six planets, four stony and two gas giants. Range is too extreme to be certain, but there is a chance that one or more might be habitable."

"Life forms?"

"Cannot reliably evaluate," came the Vulcan's immediate response.

"Uhura," barked Kirk, "any radio signals? Anything on the bands we can still monitor?"

"Nothing, sir."

"How far, at maximum impulse power, to this system, Mr. Sulu?"

"Working on it, sir. Got it." The Oriental turned in his

seat and smiled broadly. "Three days at maximum impulse power."

"Good. Lay in a course, Mr. Chekov. Get us there." Kirk watched the activity flourish around him. They again had a purpose. They forgot the touchy question of the Ammdon diplomatic mission. This was the crew he'd trained and this was the crew that he took such pride in. His finger stabbed down onto the call button. "Bones, meet me on deck four for an informal inspection." He heard the beginning of the doctor's squawk of protest, smiled and released the button, shutting off any real argument.

This was more like it. One last glance at their destination, twinkling through the cloud of cosmic dust, and then James Kirk went to meet McCoy. An inspection tour might keep the doctor busy enough to forget to complain.

"I've got things to do, Jim, important things. This is a waste of time." Leonard McCoy paced back and forth in front of his desk, hands clasped behind his back. "With the power cut to half—half!—I hardly have enough juice to keep the equipment in the surgery at functional capacity."

"I'll talk to Spock, in case you do need more. You don't have any patients at the moment, do you?"

"None, now that Chief Andres is back at work. A miracle, though. I expected everyone to come in here fried like good ole country chicken after you let the engines fall apart like that. Radiation." The man shivered. "It ought to be done away with."

Kirk ignored the doctor's outburst. It did no good trying to reason with him on some points, and McCoy hardly meant what he said. He enjoyed spouting off and releasing some of the pent-up nervousness they all felt. This was as harmless a way as any, and Kirk put up with it.

"I need your talents as a doctor. Not of the body but of the mind. I want you to accompany me and give me a report on the mental status of the crew after the accident."

"I don't need to make any damn-fool trip around looking into the crew's brains. I can tell you all you need to know."

Kirk waited. He knew McCoy would unleash a tirade on any topic, given the chance. It surprised him when it didn't come this time.

"What's your evaluation, Bones?" he asked finally.

McCoy shook his head. "Not good. This ship's morale has never been lower. If I were an independent observer from Starfleet brought in to do a full status report, I'd flunk the *Enterprise* and just about everyone aboard it."

"Just about everyone?"

"Except for Spock, dammit." That admission cost McCoy a little pride. "He seems indestructible. That half-Vulcan, half-human mix works for him in situations that push the rest of us over the edge."

"Are you in any danger of becoming a space case?"

"Hardly," the doctor snorted. "But the others I've seen are. You should have listened to me when I told you to turn back, to forget this Ammdon business."

"So you think that's at the heart of it." Kirk sucked in his breath, then let it out slowly. Spock's warnings concerning Lorelei's effect on the crew had proven too accurate; in spite of this, he still fought mental battles with himself over the alien presence. She looked so innocuous that he put little credence in the powers Spock attributed to her. But facts built up until he had to face them, no matter how reluctantly. The idea that he continually put off speaking with her on the subject told worlds. He had a vague uneasiness she was as dangerous as his science officer claimed, but he hated to admit it.

"Let's look over the crew, firsthand," he suggested. "And if you don't mind accompanying me, Bones, we can get it over with all the sooner."

"Are you going down to the engine room?"

"It's still flooded with radiation. I only intend checking the crew on the upper decks."

"In that case, I'll go. I need to stretch my legs." McCoy walked through the door and into the corridor without once looking back. He strode off but stopped less than twenty paces down the hall. Low murmurs were picked up and magnified by the metal deck plates. Kirk caught up with the doctor, then stood straining to make sense from the words.

". . . refuse to do anything. Then they'll have to return to base."

"It's war if we don't," came the response.

Kirk frowned as McCoy pointed to the recreation area. He hated himself for spying like this but had to do it. The starship captain moved up to a spot beside the blocked-open door and leaned against the bulkhead, listening.

The voices continued their earnest discussion. "We ought never to have left starbase. It was a war mission from the very beginning. It's all so clear now. We're supposed to promote peace."

"I didn't report to work. Let's see how they keep the phasers primed now!"

Kirk spun through the doorway and confronted the two. A man and a woman sat, drinking coffee, looking worried. He stormed over to them and demanded, "Why aren't you on duty? Ross and Kesselmann, isn't it?"

"Aye, sir," said the woman. She didn't bother to even rise to attention as her companion did. "I hereby refuse to ever again report to duty on the phasers. Those are weapons of war. I want only peace for everyone in the universe."

"Ensign Ross, would you consider this an adequate response in the face of Romulan aggression?"

"If we won't fight, they won't," she shot back.

"Anita," hissed her companion. "Quiet."

"No, Deke, it's time that we stood up for our beliefs. Neither of us will take part in any activity that imperils another life form. The death and destruction have to stop somewhere. It might as well be with us. We have it in our power now to do something. And we will!"

"Is she speaking for you, Ensign Kesselmann? You're assigned to the biosupport division, aren't you?"

"Life is precious, sir. Y-yes, she is speaking for me. And a lot of others in the crew," the young ensign finished, blurting out the words as if they burned his tongue. Sweat beaded his forehead, showing the intense strain he felt.

"Of course life is precious. That's why our mission to Ammdon is to prevent a war." Kirk wasn't the least surprised when both Ross and Kesselmann scoffed at that. This was the single most prevalent opinion he'd ever encountered among his diverse crew. "Have you considered that you did not hold this odd belief until after you spoke with the alien Lorelei?"

"She pointed it out. The seeds of that belief were already within us. The Federation makes it sound noble, going out and seeking new life forms. But we always end up destroying them. No more."

"When have we willfully destroyed an alien race?" demanded McCoy, finally goaded into speaking. For the most part, Kirk suspected, the doctor agreed with the two ensigns, but they'd finally stepped over the bounds of fact and irritated McCoy. "I admit that we've meddled a bit in some, but destroyed? Never!"

"That meddling destroys an alien culture as surely as if we phasered them out of existence," Anita Ross protested hotly. "What difference if we mold them to our idea of culture or outright kill them? Forcing our philosophy on an alien race is as violent a course of action as orbiting a planet and systematically destroying it with photon torpedoes!"

"Since there's little need for phasers or torpedoes in our present condition, your disobedience is not a serious breach of discipline, Ensign. However, I think sitting and consuming coffee is not a productive use of your time, considering our current plight. I'll talk to your section head and have you reassigned to other duties."

"If they require violence, I refuse the duty."

"Carry on," said Kirk, pivoting and leaving the pair in the rec room. In the corridor, he slumped and looked at McCoy. "Are there others like that?"

"More than I care to think about, Jim. But there's a healthy aspect to it, this part about not wanting to kill."

"As I tried to point out to them, try explaining that to a fully armed Romulan warship ready to blast you into plasma. War is too messy not to try to avoid, but there's a point when avoiding it with too great a diligence reduces you to slavery. I believe it is time I spoke with your foundling."

"Lorelei?"

Kirk nodded and started toward the woman's quarters. He hadn't wanted this confrontation. He saw now that he could no longer avoid it. The safety of his ship mattered more than the gut-wrenching fear he felt welling up inside.

As with all other doors aboard the *Enterprise*, that leading to Lorelei's quarters had been braced half-open and then the power had been cut. When every erg produced by the impulse engines was required for life support and rocket propulsion, the luxury of the self-opening doors had to be put aside.

"Lorelei?" he called, his voice not quite quavering. Kirk

tried to get a better grip on himself. He hadn't any reason to fear her. She was not violent. Quite the contrary. Yet he did fear her. Or was it her philosophy of pacifism? Did he fear her persuasiveness? Could she totally twist about everything he had come to believe in?

"Captain Kirk—James. Please. Enter."

She sat on a low stool, trim legs thrust out in front of her and crossed at the ankles. She wore a thin dress that clung with static-electricity tenacity to the slender curves of her body. Her large brown eyes made her look soft, young, vulnerable. The childlike qualities of her figure added to the impression. Kirk fought down a feeling of protectiveness toward her. If anything, she was more in control of the situation than he was.

"I want to ask you not to speak with any of the crew." There. He'd got it all out in one quick sentence.

"No? Am I such a subversive? My ideas are potent if you think they are the root of your problems." She leaned back, balancing herself on her hands. For a woman who appeared older, this would have been a provocative pose. Kirk found himself struck even more by the childlike quality Lorelei exuded.

"Their words sound a good deal like yours. Somehow—and I don't know how you've done it—you've put your thoughts into their heads. Many of the crew refuse to report for duty because of their newfound pacifistic ideals. If they refuse orders at a crucial moment, whether it's against a Romulan cruiser or an asteroid too large for our deflector screens to handle, not only their own lives will be forfeit but also those of everyone else about the *Enterprise*. You don't want those deaths on your conscience, do you?"

Sadness crossed the woman's face, almost as if a cloud had blanked out the disk of the sun. She shook her head. "It is not so easy, James. Ideas are insidious. Once planted, they grow and can never be eradicated. There is no turning back."

"How do you do it? Why?" He sat across from her, elbows braced on his knees. Studying her gave no hint to her motives.

"I am a Speaker of Hyla. I am taught to choose words carefully, to tend to meanings, both overt and subtle. Perhaps the subtly phrased sentence is the most important because it triggers the thought process in the listener. I did not wish to harm you or the functioning of your precious vessel. But your mission runs counter to all that I hold to be sacred."

"Over and over I hear my crew saying we go to Ammdon to start a war. That is not and never has been the Federation's purpose in sending the diplomatic mission. Ambassador Zarv and the others want peace, not war."

"Your ambassador is a remarkable Speaker. He would gain much honor on Hyla." Lorelei sighed and turned to one side, again a move that would have been sexually provocative if she hadn't appeared to be a young girl physically.

"The Romulans want this war, not the Federation."

"Yes, James, I believe that. I truly do. I have examined your records, and, while it is impossible for me to view every single item, your history is one of seeking peace and not war."

"Then why oppose us?"

"The Federation's motives are peaceful, but the tool it has chosen is the wrong one. On Hyla we learned many thousands of years ago that pure motives are meaningless without effective action. Zarv might sway Ammdon and Jurnamoria and prevent the war you fear. He is that good. But the presence of the *Enterprise* will go against this goal. Those of Ammdon are cunning."

"And they'll use the *Enterprise* to launch a strike against

Jurnamoria, who must then appeal to the Romulans for aid. I've heard it all. I must trust Zarv and Lorritson and Mek Jokkor. I . . . I'm not a diplomat. Their ways are strange to me, for the most part."

"But you are not a soldier, either. You truly desire peace. Your primary mission is to discover new worlds, contact new life forms—peacefully. *This* is a worthy profession and one you are admirably suited for."

She rose in a liquid motion and dropped to her knees in front of Kirk. A slender hand reached out and lightly brushed his flushed cheek. He stared down into the limpid pools of her chocolate-colored eyes and felt himself becoming lost. The attraction he felt for Lorelei mounted. It wasn't—quite—sexual, and yet it was, also. She embodied all that was pure and innocent and peaceful in the universe, all that was tranquil and content.

"We of Hyla fought bitter wars hundreds of centuries ago. I have experienced those primitive feelings through a certain recording technology that your culture does not appear to have. It . . . affected me greatly. All on Hyla share my loathing for warlike instincts, and we have dedicated our lives to analyzing situations and determining potential. You are blinded, or inexperienced, or naive."

"Naive?" Kirk demanded, stung by the criticism. It was Lorelei who appeared fragile and inexperienced. "Hardly."

"Perhaps a better word is tired or exhausted in both body and spirit. You and those others aboard this vessel all seem worn. It has been too long between rests for you. It is not possible to think clearly when you are tired."

"True, but we still must complete our assignment."

"Single-minded," she said, the sadness even more apparent in her face now. "I wish that my powers were even more limited than they are. It does me no honor to disgrace you by preventing completion of your orders. We of Hyla do not have such a rigid, structured society. While we are not an anarchy, we do not have leaders in the sense you do."

"How do you provide for the common good? Not everyone can provide everything they need in a complex culture."

"Hylans require little direction. If something needs doing, and we are able, we do it. All work is honorable, as long as it helps and does not harm."

"You make it sound like a perfect society." Kirk felt himself responding to the woman, and he didn't want to. Her words wove patterns about him, imprisoning him, making him feel like a savage in the presence of a sophisticate.

"Perfect?" she said in surprise, then gave a tiny laugh that rang like silver bells in Kirk's mind. "Hardly. We are all too aware of the many flaws. Working to achieve real peace, however, gives everyone purpose."

"Everyone has to have the same definition of peace." Kirk felt himself sinking into the depths of her eyes, her intellect and arguments. What she said beguiled him. It made sense; it made perfect sense. Again she reached out and lightly touched him. He turned his face to kiss the palm of her hand.

"I wish that your ways were more peaceful," she said, the sadness spreading over her words like a thick, rich sauce. "It is as if I destroy your world, even if it is necessary."

"I've trained as a soldier, but peace is dear to me. I wish we could all be at peace, throughout the galaxy. The Romulans, the Klingons, the Federation."

She said nothing, and Kirk started to reach for her fragile cheek to touch, to caress. A strident chiming shook him from his mood.

"Captain Kirk, you're wanted on the bridge. Please respond."

Kirk rose and went to the intercom, slamming the button with the side of his hand. "Kirk here. What is it, Uhura?"

"Sir, Mr. Spock reports that the cosmic dust obscuring the star system has been left behind us. He has completed his preliminary scan of the system."

"Good."

"It's even better, sir. The fourth planet in the system is inhabited."

"I'll be right up." Kirk glanced over his shoulder at Lorelei, who sat in the same motionless pose she had held since kneeling in front of him. "I've got to go," he said to her. Deep down inside, emotions churned and boiled, threatening to confuse him again. When he'd spoken with Lorelei, everything had been so pellucid. Now the words jumbled about him. Peace. War. The boundaries were no longer clear-cut.

"Go. Do your duty," she said. "And I shall do mine. That is our destiny, James. Each must do what is necessary."

He nodded, glad to leave. He hurried for the turbolift, eager to reach the bridge.

An inhabited planet! They weren't lost yet!

# Chapter Six

*Captain's Log,* Stardate 4903.01

> We will soon attain orbit about the fourth planet in the system. Uhura reports no radio signals emanating from the planet, but Mr. Spock's life-form readings indicate a highly complex civilization. The riddle posed by this seeming contradiction is only one of the items on our agenda. Nowhere in the galaxy has an advanced civilization been found that did not employ hertzian radio, even for minor communications. Perhaps this is the first.

"Assume standard orbit," Kirk commanded. Chekov and Sulu worked at their consoles to obey. Behind him Kirk heard Lieutenant Uhura scanning through every conceivable communication frequency, to no avail. "Mr. Spock, what is your impression of the world below?" He studied the vast sprawl of the browns and greens and blues shown on the viewscreen as he listened.

"Definitely advanced civilization, perhaps equal to our own."

"Space travel? Faster-than-light drives?" he demanded.

"No indication of any off-planet activity, sir. Nor is there any radiation emission in the standard communication bands. I do find, however, evidence of atomic-fission plants, involved transport systems on the planetary surface and even aerial vehicles approximating those of your twenty-first century."

"Don't you find it odd that they don't use radio?"

"I can theorize a culture lacking such. For instance, by the mid-twentieth century on Earth, little broadcast radiation leaked into space. Low-power geosynchronous communications satellites assumed an increasing burden of audio and video traffic. By the end of that century, lasers and the comsats were the primary relay methods. These, as you know, permit no leakage."

"Sulu, any evidence of comsats in orbit around the planet?"

"None, sir," came the immediate answer. "That was the first thing Mr. Spock asked me to search for."

Kirk smiled to himself. Spock seldom missed anything of real importance. That was why he consistently ranked as the best science officer in Starfleet. Kirk pushed away the idea of how much he'd be missed aboard the *Enterprise* when Spock earned a promotion to ship's captain and had his own command one day.

"How do you explain this discrepancy? According to Proctor's theory of civilizations, it isn't possible to develop a complex culture without an advanced communications network."

"I agree with the theory. I surmise that the people on the planet below employ some method of which we are ignorant. They are advanced; they might be more advanced than we."

"But they don't have space travel. Not even to their nearby planets."

"Some cultures feel no need to explore the cosmos. This might be one." Spock continued working on his computer console even as he reported. "I have detected other examples of advanced status. Their agricultural patterns are definitely those of a society at peace and with highly developed biology. Waterways indicate optimal planning for irrigation, and the surface-transport system is sufficient for distributing the crops across the planet."

Kirk allowed the viewscreen to change, increasing magnification. Spock's conclusions were based on computer-enhanced pictures, but much of what he reported was readily apparent even to Kirk's untrained eye. The fields paraded by in distinctly laid out patterns favored by farmers on most worlds; those had been selected by computers to maximize yield. He wondered if the people below also used computer analysis or if they had arrived at this in some other way.

"Now, there's a world I wouldn't mind settlin' down on," said McCoy, at Kirk's elbow. The captain jumped, not having heard the doctor approach. "Peaceful down there. A fellow can run his fingers through the soil and feel a part of nature."

"I sometimes wonder if you ever saw the outside of a farmhouse. I have this picture of you living in an Atlanta penthouse, peering out across the horizon where the fields ought to be."

"I grew up on a farm, Jim." The hurt in McCoy's voice made Kirk change the subject.

"Have you finished bioscan analysis?"

"All done and fed into Spock's computer. That planet's as near Earth norm as you'll find in all of space. A beautiful place. No pollutants in the air from factories, weather nicely controlled, the whole place approaches paradise."

"No factories? Spock, is that so?"

"Yes, Captain. Fascinating. I had not considered this aspect until now. All polluting industry is in orbit now so that Earth's atmosphere remains untainted. I find no evidence of similar orbiting factories. I am at a loss to explain the lack of atmospheric pollution."

"They might be even more advanced than we can know," mused Kirk.

"Bioscans are continuing, aimed at one of their cities," said McCoy. "Their cities are the model of efficiency, too. No grid pattern for them. That's not esthetic enough."

"There seems to be a definite predilection for the hexagon in both their architecture and their city planning. It is as efficient a pattern as the square and is more mathematically pleasing."

"He can't even find pleasure in architecture. He's got to reduce everything down to geometry and mathematical proofs."

"Doctor, I fail to see why you denigrate such logical tools. Surely it is a better way of approaching a problem than blundering through blindly as you do, relying solely on faulty emotions."

"Enough," said Kirk, silencing the two antagonists. "I don't want to beam down in the center of a city without announcing ourselves. Do you think they've discovered us orbiting their planet?"

"Negative, Captain," said Uhura. "I have been monitoring all radar and other detection bands. They don't seem to use radar, either. Any sighting of us would have to be visual, as we occlude a star."

"But how do they guide their airplanes? Tight-beamed lasers? Comments, Spock, Uhura?"

Before either could answer, an all-too-familiar voice filled the bridge. "I demand to know the meaning of this outrage."

"Ambassador Zarv, please return to your quarters. We are busy with more pressing matters than any you can contribute." Kirk felt mounting irritation at the Tellarite. He hadn't swayed the crew as Kirk had intended, although Lorelei had highly praised the diplomat's histrionic abilities. All Zarv had done was create havoc wherever he went. Kirk had to believe, in part, that the problems aboard the *Enterprise* were due to the negotiating team's presence—and attitude. If they'd stayed in their quarters, feelings wouldn't have mounted against them. Zarv rubbed everyone the wrong way.

"I shall do no such thing, Kirk. Why do we spin about this worthless ball of mud? It isn't Ammdon. I know. I've been there, and those continents are different." He waved a pudgy hand at the viewscreen.

"In case you missed it, Ambassador, our warp engines are shut down and we are in dire straits. There is no easy way of alerting Starbase One of our plight. All five of our message packets were destroyed, and without warp-engine power, we cannot use the subspace radio. We can make only limited use of our transporter. Therefore, on impulse power only it would take us years—"

"Four hundred seventy three point nine two three, to be exact," furnished Spock.

". . . almost five hundred years to return to base. Ammdon is a bit closer."

"Eighty-eight point six six six years, if the sidereal tables supplied by Ammdon astronomers are accurate."

"Thank you, Mr. Spock." Kirk's irritation rose with even his science officer. He felt pulled tight and ready to break.

"We can neither continue nor return, nor can we contact Starfleet. Therefore, our only course of action is to repair our engines. In such a case, we might be able to finish our trip to Ammdon or, if the engines are not completely fixed, use the subspace radio to report position and condition. I do not see you contributing to a solution in either instance, Ambassador. Return to your quarters and stay there."

"Kirk, I won't have you ordering me about like this. I—"

"Lieutenant Patten," Kirk called, punching his intercom button on the arm of his seat, "send five security personnel to the bridge to escort Ambassador Zarv to his quarters."

"This is an outrage!" protested Zarv, but the sight of the security team caused him to snort, spin and stalk off, flanked by the armed men.

"Mister Spock, why hasn't this planet been cataloged? An obviously advanced civilization shouldn't have gone undetected by Federation scouts." Kirk relaxed a little now that the Tellarite ambassador had been removed. In spite of their dangerous position, he felt more at home dealing with problems concerning his ship and crew than he did with recalcitrant diplomats.

"Unknown, sir. This star system is not too far from the Starbase One–Ammdon route. Certainly traffic along this path has increased after Romulan incursions began. Even behind the obscuring dust cloud, some evidence ought to have been noted."

"Perhaps no one bothered to do more than monitor radio and subspace channels, Mr. Spock," suggested Uhura. "Before being assigned to the *Enterprise* I worked on a scout ship. We often hurried through a sector, mapping only the stars with likely Class M planets, and those we always scanned for radio activity first."

"Shoddy procedure," muttered Spock.

"But sometimes necessary," Kirk said. "The galaxy is big and there will always be systems right on our doorstep that we've overlooked. Let's hope that this planet works out for our benefit."

The door to the turboelevator opened. Kirk stiffened slightly, thinking Zarv had returned. He looked back and immediately relaxed. Dr. McCoy strode up, clipboard in hand.

"Got the life-sensor readings analyzed, Jim. It looks like good news. Those people down there aren't human, but they register more so than does Spock."

"Atmosphere, aquasphere, the entire ecosphere, any problems for us?"

"Difficult to say without samples to study, but I'd say this was a prime planet, just about tailored for humans like us—or aliens like them down there." He used his clipboard to point at the viewscreen. "Outwardly humanoid, some slight deviations. Some oddities, but nothing outrageously dangerous."

"Be more specific in your report, Doctor." Spock glanced over McCoy's shoulder at the clipboard containing the preliminary results. "What do you consider an 'oddity'?"

"Well, nothing I can put my finger on. Just feelings, like the ones you're always wishing you had and don't. There's too much life down there."

"I do not wish to be hindered by your human emotions. And I do not understand what you mean by 'too much life,' Doctor."

"I don't, either, Bones." Kirk looked up at his friend.

The doctor shrugged and said, "Seems like too high a life-form reading for the number of people sampled. Might be they're more intense."

"How unscientific," scoffed Spock.

"But no one has discovered any threat, either biological

or otherwise? Mr. Spock, Bones, get a security team together and beam down."

"Aye, aye, sir." Spock was already on his way to the transporter. McCoy followed, looking more reluctant.

"You know what we want. Negotiate for the shielding. Lead if they can supply it. Anything better if they've developed it. And solid rock if there's no hope of anything else."

"Since they employ fission reactors on a wide scale, such shielding is logically an available commodity."

"What would they want in return?" asked McCoy. "Without a proper contact team, we can't offer them any of our technology, and they're advanced enough that they won't want glass beads and trinkets."

"Doctor," said Spock, "I believe the Starfleet Regulations are specific on this point. As we are endangered, our mission is in jeopardy and there is a distinct potential for greater harm when the Romulans are considered, Standing Order One is modifiable so that we can offer items not in this culture. We must be cautious in the items or knowledge offered for trade, but our actions do have the sanction of law."

"Makes me feel damn good," protested McCoy. He stared at the transporter platform and added, "That makes me feel damned good, too."

"Good luck. Keep a complete tricorder record of your meeting. The Federation Contact Department will be very interested. This is the first truly advanced technological culture discovered in more than twenty years."

"All ready, Captain," came Spock's level voice from the transporter platform. Surrounding him and McCoy were four security men.

"Activate transporter," ordered Kirk. Shimmering columns of energy formed around each of the men. They vanished from sight. Kirk wished he could be with them, but of course that wasn't possible. He was captain of a starship; his duty lay aboard his vessel. He hurried back to the bridge to monitor their first contact.

Leonard McCoy stumbled and fell to one knee, cursing. "When will they design a machine that works like it's supposed to? Damned thing dropped me an inch too far off the ground."

"You positioned yourself off balance while still aboard the *Enterprise,*" said Spock. "If you would not fear the transporter, such occurrences wouldn't happen."

"Why shouldn't I fear it? Kyle said it was being modified because of the power situation. Damn thing rips apart all my atoms, juggles them like some performer at a circus, then tosses them back together who knows where. A miracle all my enzymes are still functioning. That'd be something to look into. If you use a transporter very much, are enzyme levels affected adversely?"

"Doctor, such studies have been done on Vulcan and elsewhere and indicate no deleterious effects caused by the action of the transporter beam."

"Sir," said Neal, commander of the security team. He indicated several humanoids approaching.

Spock studied them carefully, his tricorder working the while. He and the others had beamed down on the outskirts of a large city. Soft, velvety green turf under their feet spread out as far as the city streets, which appeared to be a more familiar glossy black glasphalt power strip. Buildings nearby had the same soft texture to them; nowhere did Spock see the hardness of brick or steel in construction.

"Peculiar life-form readings," he muttered. "Most intense, as you mentioned previously, Dr. McCoy."

The humanoids drew nearer, then stopped. Hairless heads gleamed in the dim afternoon sunlight. The effect of no eyebrows caused their eyes to appear larger than human norm, but the lack of ears came to Spock as the most striking difference. The aliens stood equidistant apart, not talking, not looking at one another. They studied Spock, McCoy and the others with no discernible expression, either of curiosity or of fear.

"How do we approach them?" asked McCoy. "I haven't read *Robinson Crusoe* in a long time."

Spock stepped forward and said, "I am science officer of the starship *Enterprise* now orbiting your world. We desire commerce." No response. Spock fiddled with his tricorder, then tried once more. No visible emotion crossed the faces.

"You're a real crowd pleaser, Spock. I'm not getting any new life-form readings. You're not much good as a standup comic."

"Your ridicule is misplaced, Doctor. I get no indication from them that they even notice us. Telepathy is not unknown. Their lack of ears indicates communication other than we employ."

"Are you going to try the Vulcan mind meld?"

"I must attempt it, though it does not seem a fruitful approach at this point of contact."

Spock stepped forward, hesitated, then took another few steps to stand before the humanoid on the extreme left. The Vulcan reached out. The humanoid didn't stir. Spock touched fingers to the humanoid's forehead; the response was instantaneous.

A heavy fist lashed out and struck the Vulcan in the stomach. He staggered back, trying to recover balance and breath. He gasped out to the security team, "Wait! Don't fire!"

His voice wasn't strong enough for them to hear and obey. They fired phasers, set on stun. The humanoids trembled under the energy onslaught but didn't fall unconscious.

"Their nervous systems must not be the same," yelled McCoy. "Don't try the phasers."

By this time Spock had recovered, but nothing he could do prevented the humanoids from surging forward and seizing the security team. From thin air appeared more and more aliens until the entire landing party had been seized and subdued.

"A fine mess this is," grumbled McCoy. "Now how are you going to get us out?"

"I see no logical course of action to follow except to submit and wait for a chance to speak with those in power. Rather, to communicate in some fashion with their leaders."

"Fat chance we're going to see the light of day again," said McCoy as they were dragged along the soft green velvety turf underfoot and toward the bowels of the city.

"They were taken prisoner, sir," came Chekov's immediate report. "What action do we take?"

"Prisoner? What happened? I came straight from the transporter room. They haven't had time to get into trouble."

"Sir!" barked Chekov. "Mr. Spock attempted to communicate using Wulcan mind-merging techniques. He was struck. Security team opened fire with hand phasers. All were grabbed and taken into city."

"Sulu, any activity in orbit or near space?"

"None, Captain."

"Uhura, radio messages?"

"Negative, sir."

"Put the full tricorder tapes onto the forward viewscreen. I want to see whatever Spock and McCoy saw prior to the incident."

Kirk watched the few minutes replayed. He shook his head. It seemed improbable that such a disaster had struck without warning. Spock had approached slowly, intent clear. If he was correct about telepathy being the method of communication, it explained much. A telepathic culture needed radios the way outer space needed more vacuum; but if they were telepathic, why hadn't they read his peaceful intent? Some cultures had taboos against touching, but Spock's appearance indicated an alien presence and he had not abruptly forced himself on the humanoid. If touching was forbidden, why hadn't the humanoid backed away or otherwise indicated that Spock should halt?

"Dammit," he said, fists tightened into straining balls, "they followed first-contact procedures. That shouldn't have happened."

"What do we do, sir?" asked Chekov.

"Ready phasers. Shift energy from all level-six and lower priority items."

"Photon torpedoes also, Captain?"

"No, Mr. Chekov. The phasers are more precise. I don't want to start a war. I want to get radiation shielding from those people down there. This is not an armed aggression. Not yet."

Kirk watched as Chekov began flipping switches and getting back ready lights indicating the phasers were powering up and getting readied for action. Then red lights blossomed like flowers in the spring.

"Sir, phaser crews are not at their posts."

"Why not?"

Pavel Chekov turned and shrugged, indicating he had no idea.

"Mr. Sulu, you have the conn. I'm going to see about those crews personally. You will not open fire unless the landing party is in danger of losing their lives."

"Aye, aye, sir." Sulu slipped into the command seat as Kirk rushed to the turboelevator. He whished down and across the broad dish of the main portion of the *Enterprise* and hurried out toward the fire-control nodule fastened under the structure.

Empty. The room had been evacuated as if there'd been an alarm.

He slipped into a seat and prepared the phasers. "Mr. Sulu, status."

"Nothing has changed, sir. The aliens have penned up the landing party as if they were farm animals. They didn't even put them into a prison cell. It looks like a corral with a three-meter-high fence."

"I've activated the phaser firing circuits. Get a security force down here on the double. I want a crew manning the phasers immediately, and then I want the names of whoever abandoned this post. They are to be put on report immediately, pending further disciplinary action."

He savagely cut the intercom link with the bridge and turned his attention to readying the phasers. When light footsteps sounded behind him, he said, "Take over. I have to return to the bridge." Kirk spun in the seat and saw Lorelei standing quietly in the door.

"James, the crew has finally discovered the True Path. None will man your weapons. They have discovered a way better than violence."

"Spock, McCoy and four others are in danger below. Use of our phasers might be the only way of getting them free. Are you willing to condemn them to death?"

"If it means exchanging their lives for others, yes. Such trades are never worthwhile."

"Those are my friends, my crew members!" Kirk cried.

"It is unfortunate such a situation has arisen, but violence will not solve the problems. Violence will only aggravate an already tense condition."

"You talked my crew into abandoning their posts?"

"James, I will not lie to you. I spoke earnestly with many of them, answered their questions, eased their doubts. None will return to do harm to other living creatures. You must seek out another—a peaceful—solution."

"Security!" he said forcefully. "Show Lorelei to her quarters and see that she stays there. You, take over phaser bank one. You, man the second bank." He didn't wait to see if his orders were being carried out or not. Those in security weren't easily swayed by arguments. They knew their duty and performed it well.

As did Captain James T. Kirk.

Yet, as he returned to the bridge, Lorelei's words gnawed away at his rock-solid mental defenses. What if she were right? What if there were a way that didn't involve using force?

He shook himself angrily. "I'll explore all peaceful ways before using the phasers. That's the way I've been trained, that's the way I believe."

Still, Kirk found himself doubting even as he resumed his command seat on the bridge.

Stickiness penetrated his tunic and turned his skin tacky. Startled, Kirk turned to see Mek Jokkor standing beside him. The alien's expression was one of consternation. He was as upset as Kirk had ever seen him. The hand tightened and tiny prickly tendrils danced across sensitive skin. Kirk guessed it was the plant man's way of communicating; to him it meant nothing.

"I'm sorry, I don't understand."

"There's much you do not understand, you raving space

worm!" Ambassador Zarv thundered onto the bridge, trailing Donald Lorritson behind. "Is it true that you've lost your science officer in an abortive attempt to talk those bumpkins out of a few cubic meters of radiation shielding?"

"I have not lost my science officer, as you put it, Ambassador. He, Dr. McCoy and four others have been taken prisoner by the inhabitants of this planet. We have been unable to figure out what taboos were broken to cause such action on the natives' part."

"Amateurs. They are all amateurs in Starfleet. I sometimes wonder why I remain in the Federation diplomatic service."

"Captain," said Lorritson, cutting past his superior's tirade, "we have examined the tricorder tapes and cannot discern any reason for the action taken by the natives. However, the tricorder does not record subtleties we are trained to observe. Small facial twitches, slight movement, even the relative distances between personnel. Millions of data are our stock-in-trade."

"Get to the point, Mr. Lorritson."

"We wish to beam down and arrange for the release of your crew members. In the process, we feel it possible to obtain the radiation shielding required to repair the *Enterprise*."

Kirk considered this for a moment. The offer seemed reasonable enough. These three were trained negotiators. Let them get Spock and McCoy and the others out of hot water. Zarv, Lorritson and Mek Jokkor knew the ropes, knew how to get things peacefully. They wouldn't require the use of force to back them up. That was the only way: peacefully.

He shook his head, as if to clear cobwebs in it. The words echoing inside his skull sounded precisely like those

Lorelei had uttered. Insidiously she had intertwined her thoughts with his and blurred the decisions he had to make. He wanted a quiet settlement of this problem, but he could not rule out force if it became necessary.

Unlike Lorelei, he believed force sometimes *did* solve problems. It was to be regretted, but force sometimes held the answer to otherwise intractable dilemmas.

"I appreciate your offer, Mr. Lorritson, but I cannot take the risk of sending another party down immediately. A second group, following on the heels of the first, might incite the natives. We will try to figure out what happened; then one of you will be permitted to accompany the second party. As a group, you three are too valuable to risk."

"We work as a team, Kirk." Zarv's belligerence increased. "You got us into this mess. We do no good sitting on our thumbs. Let us get your crew free and get us on our way. We have to be in the Ammdon council chambers in less than two weeks. If we fail to arrive, war is the only possible outcome."

"If you're tossed into the prison corral with Spock and the others, you'll never make it to Ammdon. Your safety is my responsibility, Ambassador, whether you like it or not. Please present an analysis of the situation for my evaluation. Lieutenant Avitts will run your findings through the computer." He pointed to the woman at Spock's station. While she wasn't as able as Spock—who in all of Starfleet was?—she had learned much from him. She'd perform as well as anyone could under the circumstances.

"We have no time for such time-wasting maneuvers. We will not form a committee to study forming a committee, Kirk. That's for seatbound bureaucrats. We must go to the planet's surface and have a face-to-face meeting with their leaders."

"We haven't even identified their leaders, Zarv," Kirk said, his patience wearing thin.

"We can have this misunderstanding cleared up quickly, Captain," cut in Donald Lorritson. The man smoothed his impeccable red silk doublet, picking off imaginary specks of lint. "It is what we have been trained to do."

"This 'misunderstanding' is more fundamental than my officers' ineptness in alien contact, Mr. Lorritson. You have heard my orders. Carry them out."

"Orders!" roared Zarv. "We are not under your orders. We are . . ."

Lorritson and Mek Jokkor both took their ambassador aside, and the human spoke earnestly with the Tellarite for several minutes. Mek Jokkor stood to one side, appearing to take no further interest in the discussion. Kirk couldn't help but wonder at Mek Jokkor's thought processes. How did a plant relate to animal life? Did it seem silly and abrupt, or merely tolerable? There wasn't any way of finding out. Not now. Perhaps later Kirk might ask, when things had returned to a more peaceful norm.

"Very well, Captain," snorted Zarv. The trio left without further ado.

"Whew," said Kirk, slumping down in his seat. "I'm glad to see the last of them for a while. Chekov, report. What condition are the phasers in?"

"Uh, sir. No one responds when I call."

"Have you taken control?"

"Of course, sir, but some switching is required. I cannot do it all from this position. Some crew need be at the station."

More abandonment of position. His crew had been more influenced by Lorelei than he'd dare admit to himself. One good round with the phasers was all he could count on. He hoped it wouldn't come to that.

"Sir?" came Uhura's sharp query. "Did you authorize use of the transporter?"

"Of course not. What's going on?"

"Zarv and his assistants just beamed down, sir. They're on the planet's surface."

The sinking feeling Kirk experienced intensified. The diplomats had disobeyed his orders.

# Chapter Seven

*Captain's Log,* Stardate 4904.2

Spock, McCoy and four security men are imprisoned on the planet below. To make matters worse, Ambassador Zarv and his diplomatic mission beamed down to the planet without permission; the diversion of power required for this use of the transporter necessitated entirely closing down level seven. Only when we regain some measure of warp-engine power will we be able to use this area again. Contact with the civilization inhabiting the planet grows increasingly less likely. If, as Spock inferred, the natives employ a form of telepathy, there is scant chance of our success in negotiating either for the release of those imprisoned or for the shielding we so desperately need.

"Captain, I have contact with the ambassador. None took a communicator; this is a patch through the video portion of a tricorder." Uhura punched in the proper combination and the forward viewscreen scrambled, to re-form in the image of the Tellarite diplomat.

Kirk did not allow Zarv a chance to speak. He immediately said, "You beamed down without my permission. I am still captain of this starship. Prepare to beam back immediately. You are in grave danger."

"We are in no danger, Kirk. We are diplomats. We know how to contact and deal with other cultures. Unlike your blundering fools, we have established a working rapport."

Zarv turned and indicated Mek Jokkor standing on the velvety green turf, feet widespread and an expression of sheer bliss on his face. Kirk watched as the alien's features began to flow, to alter into something less human in form. Mek Jokkor returned to his natural plantlike shape, leafy hands lightly fluttering in the soft breeze blowing from the countryside toward the city.

"See? He is making good progress. While no telepath, he communicates in other nonverbal ways. We will make progress. We will obtain the release of your officers *and* get the materiel you need to get us on our way to Ammdon."

"You're dealing with a society totally unlike any we've found before. Spock is no fool. He wouldn't—" Kirk didn't have the chance to finish his warning. Mek Jokkor stiffened and twisted. His feet had taken root in the soil beneath the turf. Rising up to twine about his legs came brown snakes, slithering and biting. The plant man jerked and tried to pull free. The snakes circled and moved upward, sending him to his knees. No sound echoed from his mock mouth. That made the scene all the more terrible. Mek Jokkor was in terrible pain and was unable to give voice to it.

"Don't touch him, Zarv!" Kirk barked. But it was too

late. The Tellarite rushed to aid his assistant, to pull free the brown bands working up Mek Jokkor's body. The instant the ambassador touched one of the snakes, the humanoids watching were galvanized into action. They seized Zarv and began dragging him off. Donald Lorritson stood open-mouthed—and unharmed.

"I don't understand," Lorritson muttered into his communicator. "What's happening? Why are they attacking?"

"They haven't noticed you. Keep it that way. Prepare to beam up. I'll have the power diverted. We'll try to pick up the ambassador and Mek Jokkor later."

"I can make them listen."

"They're telepaths, Lorritson. Don't try meddling. Mek Jokkor did something to anger them. The ambassador intervened. Don't try anything that'll get you noticed by them." Of Sulu he asked, "Is power back on the transporter?"

"Sir, switching is difficult. Mr. Scott just gave me additional energy from the impulse engines for maintaining orbit. It has to be recircuited."

"Do it, dammit!"

"Aye, aye, sir."

Kirk fumed as he watched the scene unfolding on the planet below. Lorritson's tricorder continued to monitor faithfully the capture of Mek Jokkor and Zarv. The humanoids dragged the struggling pair toward the town, no doubt to be imprisoned with Spock and the others.

"Lorritson, don't! There's nothing you can do to help!" Kirk cried. The diplomat ignored him and raced for the tight knot of humanoids. The starship captain watched in helpless rage as Lorritson bodily tackled the nearest native, knocking him spinning. From out of range of the diplomat's tricorder, now discarded and on the ground, came the sounds of pounding feet. Animals mixing the worst aspects of Terran gorillas and Vegan sundevils surrounded the group.

Struggles ceased.

The last glimpse Kirk got was of Lorritson being dragged, unconscious, in the direction of the city.

"Sulu, any luck yet getting power reestablished in the transporter unit?"

"Bad luck, sir. The range-finding unit has been destroyed by a power surge during switching."

Kirk tensed, fingers clutching the armrests of his command seat. Without the range finder they'd be unable to beam up any of those on the ground who did not have communicators tuned to the proper frequency. And Spock and the others had lost their communicators, either through search or during the heat of battle. Zarv and Mek Jokkor hadn't had communicators, and Lorritson's tricorder now lay on the ground, useless for the purpose of pinpointing location.

"Any way of using the transporter without the range finder or a communicator linkup?"

"Sir," Sulu said skeptically, "if we're off the merest fraction of a nanometer, anyone in the transporter beam would be killed, their atoms jumbled up in some random pattern. The range-finder unit is vital—or they need a communicator for us to lock on to. Either one works. But to just try grabbing . . ."

Sulu didn't have to spell it out. Kirk had been railing against the fate that had put them all into this situation. He knew that the odds against a successful transport without precise range information were astronomical. One transport in trillions lacking the precision equipment might work. Maybe. But he didn't know anyone willing to take the risk at those improbable odds.

"Uhura, can you locate the communicator units on the planet?"

"Done, sir. They are all piled up just outside the city. I

have it on scan now." The scene showed little of interest. The distance from orbit to planet was too great, even for their sophisticated viewscreens, to make out much detail other than that the communicators were intact. Uhura altered the focus to the corral where Spock, McCoy and the others in the first feckless landing party were penned. Zarv and his aides now added to the number. They appeared unharmed in spite of their struggles.

"They must escape that pen and get to the communicators."

"How are we going to do that, Captain?" asked Chekov.

"Ready phasers. We'll burn a hole through the corral, then use intermittent phaser fire to show the path to the communicators. Spock will understand. Sulu, I want all power possible shunted into the transporter when they reach the communicators."

"We barely have enough power to run the transporter and life-support systems and maintain orbit. We'll have to constantly switch back and forth between the phasers and the transporter."

"And that's what burned out the range finder." Kirk heaved a deep sigh. He knew Scotty labored like Hercules just to keep the *Enterprise* as functional as it was. "Tell Mr. Scott to switch on command."

"Aye, aye, sir."

Kirk gazed at the viewscreen, then ordered, "Take out the northern perimeter of the corral. Phasers, fire!"

Nothing.

"Phasers, fire! What's wrong, Chekov? Fire!"

"Sir, there is no response from phaser crews."

"Keep trying. I'll see to it personally."

He swung out of his command seat, called out, "Sulu, you have the conn," then plunged down the turbolift to the phaser deck. Lights had been cut to preserve power, and the circulating fans whined at half speed. He burst into the control center and experienced a *déjà vu* sensation. Again the entire area was deserted. Again his crew had abandoned their posts. This time it meant imprisonment and possible death for Spock, McCoy, the diplomats and the security team on the planet.

"Sir, please do not touch the console." Kirk spun to see several crewmen from a security team standing along the rear bulkhead. "Use of the phasers against the society below is wrong."

"Get to your posts immediately. This is a direct order! Lives will be lost if you don't obey."

"We'd like to do as you say, sir, except it means using violence. We cannot do that. Lorelei has explained it all to us."

Kirk didn't have time to argue. He turned to the panel and began priming the phaser for firing sequence. When the lights flashed ready, he hit the intercom button. "Chekov, fire! I've got the phasers set for three-second bursts."

No answer.

"Chekov?" he called. "Answer. What's happening? Fire the phasers."

"Sir," came the hesitant voice. "I will call you back in a few minutes."

Kirk sagged as if someone had hit him with a pile driver. He regained composure, turned and said, "All of you. Out of the room. Now!" To his relief and surprise, they obeyed. He seized a hand phaser from a rack on the bulkhead and herded the security team out into the corridor. He dragged shut the door and welded a quick seam, sealing it. The phaser weld would hold against all but the most diligent of efforts to get into the room and permanently disable the controls.

"Return to your quarters until further orders," Kirk said.

He raced for the bridge, hoping that his worst fears weren't being acted out.

The instant he burst upon the bridge he knew command had slipped from his fingers. The small groups standing about talking he had fought against earlier had re-formed. They quietly discussed—what? He had the sinking feeling it was Lorelei's philosophical pacifism.

"Chekov, fire phasers!" he cried. Ensign Chekov turned and shook his head.

"Captain, I am sorry. Use of weapons is not the way of solving this problem."

"That's an order, mister. Carry it out."

Chekov shook his head again and left his post. Sulu joined him. To one side Lieutenant Avitts and Uhura were already speaking to each other, voices low and eyes occasionally directed toward Kirk. He stood stock-still, feeling like an island in the middle of a storm. Nowhere on the bridge were officers performing their duties.

On the viewscreen Kirk saw the corral, with Spock and the others penned inside. He jerked at the sight of one of the security team attempting to scale the thorn walls. The ensign reached the top, only to be impaled by a suddenly sprouting thorn as thick as a man's wrist. He stiffened, agony written on his face. Without sound, Kirk couldn't hear the death shrieks. The ensign toppled, only to hang lifeless from the immense thorn through his body.

This convinced Kirk that action had to be taken immediately. He dashed forward, pushing Chekov from his path. His finger stabbed down on the trigger button, but answering phaser fire didn't belch forth from the underside of the *Enterprise*.

"Your crew has disabled the phasers, James, in spite of your efforts to prevent it," came the soft voice. Lorelei stood in the turbolift. She walked out, graceful and childlike. But the expression on her face wasn't in the least innocent. It carried lines of worry and the burdens of a long, harsh lifetime. "I do not like doing this to you, James. Please believe me. In its way, it is aggression, but aggression without death. Your way leads only to death. Mine is softer. Pacifism is the True Path."

"Look at the viewscreen. One of my junior officers just died on that planet. Death, Lorelei, is final. He died violently when I might have prevented it. Let me blast open the thorn walls and get my crew and the diplomatic mission out. They can beam back if they reach their communicators."

"He died because he took violent action. The deadliness of his action turned against him. No, James, I cannot allow you to use the phasers against a helpless civilization."

"Lorelei, this is mutiny."

"The crew is, by your laws, in mutiny. I am not. Peace must prevail, even if it means breaking laws. There is a higher calling, and that is preservation of life. Life must take precedence over any mere man-made law."

Kirk felt the web of her words spinning about him, beguiling, warping his views. Peace was the only way. He had been wrong to order the phaser crews to action. She walked toward him, and for the first time he caught a hint of perfume from her, a fragrance that sent his head spinning. Kirk braced himself against the computer console, trying to piece together all that had happened.

Peace. War. Not war. It all jumbled together.

"I'm not a violent person," he screamed, the contradiction obvious to all on the bridge. "You're making me do this."

"You want to be peaceful, James. You can be. Put down

the phaser. Working together in harmony will get us the shielding material. Peace is always the answer, not aggressive behavior."

The words hummed with vibrant power. He felt himself beginning to believe. No, more than that. He began to *believe*. Heart and soul convinced of Lorelei's claims, he started to *believe*. Until he wrenched his head to one side and saw the lifeless form of the crewman dangling from the thorn corral, the once-red blood beginning to turn black and coagulate on the thorny tip.

*"NO!"* he roared. The surge of anger and adrenaline pushed aside the insidious effect of Lorelei's words. "Uhura, Chekov, Sulu, listen to me. We've got to save them—save ourselves!"

"Captain, she is right," spoke Uhura, her voice soft and caressing. "There are more important pursuits than aggression." Her eyes focused at some point nearer infinity than the bridge of the *Enterprise* as she added, "Did you know my name means *peace?*"

Kirk spun and slammed his hand down. Pain lanced up into his elbow. The shock jarred his shoulder and kept away Lorelei's new onslaught of enticing words. He bolted for the turboelevator.

"James, don't. There is nowhere to run. All aboard the *Enterprise* now agree with me."

"I should never have let you debate Zarv. Giving you direct contact with all the crew was a mistake."

"It was not a mistake, James. It allowed me to touch everyone—enough. Peaceful existence is never a mistake. Don't fight it so. Please," she implored. "Please."

The door hissed shut. Kirk punched the controls for the engineering deck. The *Enterprise* lay more dead than living in orbit. What life remained in her steel hull came from

Scotty's deft fingers, the way he coaxed just a bit more power from the impulse engines, the methods he used to extort energy from dying warp engines.

The warning lights had been turned off. Scotty had finally contained the radiation leakage that had made the engineering deck into a deathtrap. Kirk rushed to the door leading into the engine room and stared inside. Scotty, Chief McConel and many of the others on the engineering staff stood about, doing nothing.

"Scotty, not you, too?" he said in dismay. "I can't do it without you. I can't."

"Sair, 'tis nae right what you're doin'. Listen to the wee lass."

Fight went out of James Kirk. He had never expected Scotty to desert him. The most loyal members of his crew turned on him and listened to Lorelei's honeyed words. He had failed to deliver Zarv and his peace mission to Ammdon. He had allowed his ship to become almost totally disabled. His friends and members of the crew were imprisoned and dying on the planet below. And now his remaining crew had turned on him, mutinying even as Spock had hinted they might.

He slumped as Scotty came to stand beside him. "Captain, you're lookin' tired. We can handle it all. We can do what is necessary."

Something snapped inside him. "No! This is my ship. I will not give up command. Not to you, not to Lorelei, not to anyone. It's my responsibility, and I will not relinquish it without a fight!"

He shoved Scotty away and turned for the door. A security team blocked his path, Lorelei in front of them.

"James," she said. "Your violence is inbred to an unimaginable degree. You are upsetting the others around you and causing them to doubt the nonviolence I have taught them."

"You've brainwashed them. I don't know how, but you've turned them against me, against the Federation. They have mutinied."

"They've become more in tune with the universe around them. Rather than fighting, they merge and become unified. There is no conflict when you are part of a greater whole. There cannot be."

Kirk whipped up his phaser, but he was too late. The last he heard was Lorelei's sad words, "You're only stunned. Even this violence pains me, but it is necessary to prevent further violence."

The tingling phaser stun beam seized control of his nerves. He twitched once, then crumpled to the deck, unconscious.

From the distance came the whistle of wind through trees. A dripping noise triggered old and almost forgotten memories in Jim Kirk's mind: rain falling from leaves. He felt as if his body had rejected him; the pain lashed at his senses and forced reality upon him. He groaned and rolled over. Sunlight, warm and comforting, bathed his face. Blinking at the unexpected light, he shielded his eyes with an uplifted hand, then struggled to sit upright. Beneath him freshly fallen leaves crushed moistly and fragrantly, and the neatly cropped turf he had seen from the bridge of the *Enterprise* flowed like a liquid beneath his palms.

Kirk looked around. He had been transported to the surface of the planet.

"My communicator!" he cried, grabbing for the spot on his belt where it normally hung. It had vanished. "Lorelei exiled me to the planet." Panic rose and fell quickly as he realized how much worse his position might have been.

Lorelei might have imprisoned him aboard ship. Escaping from a detention cell was virtually impossible. This way, free on the planet, he had a chance.

"First find Spock and McCoy, then back to the *Enterprise* and my command," he vowed aloud. He rose and stood quietly, looking through the copse toward the grassy plain where the others had beamed down. Kirk hesitated and listened when rustling among the fallen leaves warned him of approaching life.

Small animals, barely larger than Terran house cats, scavenged among the leaves, rooting down and finding grubs and other insects, devouring them, then trotting on to a new location. Curious, Kirk followed and watched. Even though numerous grubs existed in each spot the animals pawed, they ate only a few before moving on. Most animals would feast until nothing remained before seeking out a new food source.

The silence began to wear on his nerves. No mating cries sounded, no hunting snarls or vigorous arguments. None of the creatures he spied had ears or, apparently, vocal cords. And none paid him the least attention. Frowning, he ventured out of the forest, then stopped. Something bothered him more than the quiet. Kirk stared into the woods, and it finally came to him.

"There's no undergrowth. No shrubs littering the forest floor. It's as neat there as if a gardener cleared it periodically." Nowhere he looked was there a plant or shrub out of place. And each growth was perfectly formed, no trace of blight or disease. "It's like a garden," he muttered as he walked on.

A group of humanoids came toward him. He debated facing them now or running for cover, such as it was in the denuded forest. Kirk finally decided that they'd spotted him and no amount of flight would prevail. He waited anxiously. And they walked past him, not even casting him a sidelong glance.

"Wait!" he called out, puzzled by this lack of reaction on their parts. "Stop!" They walked on, never breaking stride. All marched in perfect unison. Kirk chastised himself for not remembering that they had no hearing organs. All the shouting in the world would produce no effect. He began searching for Lorritson's discarded tricorder. He soon found it and switched off the transmission back to the *Enterprise*. He had no intention of letting Lorelei see what he planned.

Sitting cross-legged on the turf, he began studying the tricorder readings, trying to piece together a picture of this peculiar planet. Repeatedly he had seen the humanoids ignore strange things happening about them, only to react strongly when contact was attempted. Spock's mind-fusion attempt had set off one humanoid. Mek Jokkor had been sinking roots into the ground when the snakes attacked; the natives had joined in swiftly and in perfect unison.

"Perfect unison," he muttered, the phrase turning over and over. He began punching various possibilities into the tricorder, then checking the results as the tiny machine processed and reported findings.

"Perfect harmony," he finally said. Kirk began digging until he found rootlike tendrils a few centimeters under the surface. The tricorder purred as he ran it the length of the uncovered growths. He jumped to his feet when a small animal with a nose shaped like a spade sauntered toward him. The creature burrowed its nose into the soil and began covering the tendrils. When it had finished its task, it left as quietly as it had arrived. In a few seconds, the grass liquidly flowed back over the naked soil. No evidence of disruption remained.

"The planet is self-repairing. Everything works together.

Disturb one part, and the rest comes to its aid. That's why the scavengers in the forest didn't eat all the grubs. The grubs serve a purpose; but do some sacrifice themselves so that the scavengers can eat? Who decides what's in balance?" He clicked off the tricorder, wishing Spock were with him. Spock and Bones were the experts for an ecological puzzle like this. They'd know the answers he only fumbled at.

Kirk started for the city, careful to avoid stepping on anything that wiggled or moved. The grass was safe; its role in life was to be walked on. But the spaceman was careful not to disturb any other living being. Finding Spock became more and more important if he wanted to regain control of the *Enterprise*—and to simply survive on this planet.

# Chapter Eight

*Captain's Log,* Stardate 4905.8

> Marooned on the planet, I have few choices left to me. The crew of the *Enterprise* has mutinied, falling prey to the alien Lorelei's words of pacifism. I must reach Spock and the others, rescue them and, using this small group, regain control of my starship. The outlook for this is not good.

Jim Kirk walked as if eggshells paved the black ribbon of road leading into the city. He worried that he might disturb the careful balance he had witnessed at work out in the forest. Treading softly, avoiding the humanoid natives, not attempting contact of any sort, he made his way into the city, tricorder working the while. The readings it gave caused him to gasp in wonderment at the marvelous biology of this planet. Not only were the obvious humanoid natives ambulant and alive, so were the buildings. He hesitantly placed his hand next to a wall seemingly constructed of brick. A warm, pulsating surface greeted his touch. The planar wall buckled slightly, retreating just enough to let him know the entire building was a living, breathing entity.

He pulled back, gazing up at the top of the biologically active four-story building. Humanoids entered and left, treating this edifice as would any dweller on any other planet where it would have been built from steel and granite.

"Imagine that. They grow their buildings. Animal? Vegetable?" The tricorder did not give him the answer to the question. All he received was a strong reading indicating life. The delicate analysis of the information had to be left to those more expert.

He went back to the middle of the street and walked directly through the center of the city. On both sides towered the living buildings. Once he saw one of the buildings under "construction." Humanoids and tiny black, darting creatures similar to Altairian spider birds coaxed the building into soaring, into growing straight and true. The bird creatures laid out cobweb lines from the base to the top that the building followed with uncanny ease. Kirk watched as the building visibly grew. At first the growth amounted to only centimeters per minute, but it quickly became meters, huge lurches thrusting the structure toward the cerulean sky. The humanoid natives were neither slaves nor bosses. They labored equally with the bird creatures and, inside the sprouting building, worms gnawing through the pulpy interior to form perfectly shaped hallways and rooms.

"A symbiosis. All working together, all needing the others to survive. The perfect communism. One part relies on all others, all knowing what to do and to what extent. Fascinating." Kirk stopped and thought about what he had said. He had to laugh. "I'm beginning to sound like Spock. But it is fascinating."

Sure that the tricorder scanned and recorded the entire building process, he moved on, following a strength signal on the device indicating the direction of the imprisoned humans from the *Enterprise*.

The roadway soon turned rough underfoot. Huge black chunks of living pavement thrust up to trip him. He danced back, frowning at the ground. The paving sank back into a quiescent state. Not ten meters away rose a fence of thorns.

"Spock," he shouted. "Are you there?"

"There is no other place we can be, Captain," came the Vulcan's measured tones. "I assume you remain free. It surprises me you did not attempt to rescue us using the transporter."

"The range-finder unit was destroyed by a power surge during switching."

"And we do not have our communicators to provide accurate location data otherwise. It is as I surmised."

"Jim, can you get me out of this place? I can't stand much more of Spock. He's acting too damn superior." McCoy's voice came, peevish but not frightened.

"I wish I could. There's been some trouble aboard the ship."

A long pause from the other side of the thorn wall. McCoy said in a choked voice, "Mutiny?"

"Yes." Kirk didn't try to hide the bitterness in his voice. "None of the officers supported me. All supported Lorelei. Even Scotty and Uhura and Chekov and Sulu. All of them turned pacifist when I tried to use phasers to get you out of that corral."

"Spock thought it would happen. Damn, he was right again!"

"How can I get you out?" asked Kirk. "We can discuss getting back aboard the *Enterprise* afterward. I can't get closer than ten meters without the pavement starting to rise up and trip me."

"Dr. McCoy has advanced the only possible mode of escape, Captain," said Spock. "Do you have his medical kit with you?"

"No. If you don't have it, it must be with the communicators. The natives piled them together at the edge of town. All I've got with me is the tricorder Lorritson dropped." Kirk hesitated, then asked, "How are the diplomats?"

"Mek Jokkor is dead."

Kirk shivered, in spite of the warm breeze blowing through the city. "I watched as he attempted to put down roots and somehow angered the symbiosis."

"That is not quite accurate, Captain. A symbiosis is a composite of many smaller individual entities necessarily living together. I think this planet is more, that this entire planet is one giant, living, connected organism."

"You mean the parts don't even have to communicate? At least as one organism does with another?"

"That is the only possible explanation, Captain. Telepathy is not encompassing enough to direct the life form that constitutes this entire planet. Mek Jokkor must have been seen by the life form as an intruder little different from a cancer. Humanoids removed him . . . permanently. They gave no more thought to their actions than T-cells do in your bloodstream."

"Zarv? Lorritson?"

"They are withdrawn into a shell over the death. I believe they discuss possible ventures for diplomatic contact, but none of their schemes sounds feasible."

"What are you going to do with McCoy's medkit?"

"It contains anesthetic, Jim," came Bones's words through the thick veil of thorns. "I've examined the corral, and it's got a single root. A shot of metamorphine into the taproot will put it out of commission. While it's 'unconscious,' for want of a better term, we can push through the wall and escape. When it recovers—or if the rest of the planet senses it's gone to sleep—all hell will be out for lunch."

"It's a long shot," admitted Spock, "but it is the only logical course open to us."

"I'll get the medkit. Don't go away."

"Captain Kirk, your attempts at humor leave much to be desired."

The trip to the town's perimeter and back with the medkit took longer than Kirk had anticipated. He stuffed all the communicators into the kit, as well as Spock's tricorder and other instruments carried by the security force. He lightly touched one of the phasers, then secured it at his belt. Nothing had shown him that the weapon would be effective planetside. Sudden cessation from any portion of the single-entity organism only attracted attention, something he didn't want. There wasn't enough energy in a hand phaser to stun an entire planet. There might not be enough energy in the ship's main phaser bank for that, even if they had full power from the warp engines.

He approached the corral from a different direction. Turf, rather than the black paving, slipped under the thorn wall. As a result he got closer to the pen before the turf began to rebel and hold him at bay.

"I've got the medkit. Should I throw the bag over the wall?"

"Do so carefully. Do not touch the thorns. They are most responsive to touch."

Kirk looked up, then swallowed hard. A lump formed in his throat. Dangling above him impaled on a thick thorn was the security ensign who had attempted to go over the top. His body had begun decomposing; that didn't bother Kirk as much as the way the thornbush grew about the corpse, as if it devoured the unlucky man.

"Here it comes." He swung the medkit around his head, then loosed it at the proper instant. It flew up and over the wall. He didn't hear an impact inside. McCoy had fielded it perfectly.

"There," came the satisfied doctor's voice. "I've got enough metamorphine to put this whole damn place to bed for a week."

"Do not inject enough to shock the thornbush, Doctor," warned Spock. "Incapacity must overtake the creature too slowly to be noticed."

"You worry too much, Spock. I'm used to handling farm animals. They never knew what hit 'em when I worked on them."

"That certainly explains your bedside manner with the crew."

"Cut the chatter," said Kirk, "and get to work. I'm afraid they'll notice something's wrong and close in on us. The creatures have to be able to hear us talking."

"Doubtful, Captain. No animal or vegetable creature seen to date has ears or earflaps or other hearing organs. Deafness extends throughout all species. When the entire planet is considered as one highly integrated organism, hearing is no more required than it is necessary for your foot to hear what your arm is doing."

"The analogy is rotten, Spock," said McCoy. "My application of the tranquilizer is superb, however."

Even as he spoke, Kirk watched the vicious upthrusting thorns begin to sag slightly. The ensign's body tumbled to the ground not a meter away. By the time he was able to force himself to examine the young crewman, a way had opened in the thorn wall. Spock held rubbery thorns apart for McCoy, the three remaining security men and the two diplomats. Both Zarv and Lorritson came silently, subdued. No braggadocio, no false courage. They'd been stunned by all that had happened to them.

"They ate Mek Jokkor," muttered Lorritson as he passed through into freedom. "They ate him!"

"Rather," corrected Spock, "he was assimilated. Given a different circumstance, Mek Jokkor might have been most likely to establish rapport. He unfortunately appeared to menace the highly ordered life form of this world."

"Let's get out of here and find a safe place in the woods," said Kirk. "We've got to do some planning."

"Captain," said Spock, "one place is identical with another as far as relative safety is concerned. We are free of the corral. I suggest we not waste time. As soon as Dr. McCoy's potion wears off, an alarm will be sounded for us. If we do nothing to create a disturbance until then, we might as well stay here as be in the woods."

"It's hard believing the entire world can spy on us—or detect us."

"That is a somewhat paranoid view, but in essence it is true enough. Now tell me what happened aboard the ship."

Kirk quickly outlined all that had happened, his voice becoming brittle and his bitterness rising to the surface as he talked. He finished by saying, "I thought better of them. Especially Scotty and the bridge crew. But they were as eager as any of the others to mutiny."

"You blame them wrongly, Captain," said Spock. "Relieved of duty while incarcerated, I had the time and opportunity to consider many facets of Lorelei's presence. I surmised that she has more than histrionic talents."

"What do you mean?"

"She must be empathic. Sensing opposition, she changes the tenor of her argument until the listener is more responsive. In this fashion, she tailors the most successful argument for each person. Another aspect of this talent might be the ability to utter subsonic and ultrasonic harmonics."

"You mean she can adjust the pitch and timbre of her voice so that we don't even know it? That's pretty far-fetched," scoffed McCoy.

"It explains her ease in converting the crew of a Federation starship to her pacifistic philosophy. In a way, she has patterned an individualized hypnotic speech for each crew member. She touches lines of thought we do not even recognize we entertain, then plays on them. Perhaps these touch our deepest fears, prejudices, ideas of honor and self."

"You're saying Scotty and the others weren't acting on their own?" Kirk clutched at this straw.

"Lorelei affected them in a manner analogous to a drug in the bloodstream. The recipient is not responsible for the result; the person administering the drug is."

"You're saying she's a psychologist? That she drugs with words laced with hypnotizing harmonics? That's putting a lot onto that slip of a girl." McCoy squatted down and rummaged through his medkit, taking inventory of what he had with him.

"It explains much. I also question the idea she is a girl, as you put it. I believe her to be much older than adolescent."

"Her age isn't a matter of debate, gentlemen," cut in Kirk. "Getting off this planet and regaining command of the *Enterprise* is."

"Whatever you do, we must act quickly," spoke up Donald Lorritson. "I . . . I fear that the ambassador has been damaged." He held up his hand as McCoy started for the Tellarite. "No, not in the body. There he is sound. He comes from sturdy stock. It's his mind. Zarv has never suffered a defeat of this magnitude. The loss of a prized assistant has unnerved him, as have subsequent events." Lorritson motioned toward the thorn pen.

"He's just depressed. He'll snap out of it—if we get off this damn planet."

"Doctor, the proper term is 'when' and not 'if.' We shall soon have transport away." Spock pointed into the cloudless sky.

Kirk turned and peered into the sun. A shiny silver speck appeared, grew larger, then roared across the sky.

"A shuttle craft!"

"Precisely," said Spock. "Our way off planet. Let's hurry before we are missed."

The small party picked its way through the middle of the city, observing planetary protocol and never interrupting any creature at its duty. They reached the far side of the city and began a long trek out into the countryside.

Twice as they marched the shuttle craft left and returned. Kirk said, "Must be loading shielding. Somehow Lorelei has convinced the planetary life form to give her the shielding."

"My tricorder is picking up traces of radioactivity. One of the life form's fission-power plants is nearby."

"Where, Spock?" Kirk craned his neck. Low, rolling hills hid the horizon, but no evidence of elaborate facilities showed. "They have to supply it somehow and get the power out. There's not even much in the way of a road here, much less power lines."

"Transportation is limited, Captain. What I have seen is

organically based. Some aerial craft resemble airplanes from Earth's history, but they are organic constructs, just as the buildings are. Their resemblance is purely a matter of form being dictated by function and strict adherence to Bernoulli's equation."

"There has to be heavy concrete and lead shielding, perhaps even force screens, for an atomic-power plant," protested McCoy. "I figured that's why the shuttle is landing nearby. Shielding material is mined nearby their plant so they don't have to drag it so far."

"A logical deduction, Doctor. However, I have come to suspect that all is organically based on this planet. Even speaking of the inhabitants as 'they' might be in error."

"You're saying only one life form runs everything?"

"In the same way you are a single life form comprising mitochondria, nuclei, endoplasmic reticula, Golgi bodies, bacteria and viruses of various kinds and functions, indeed an entire army of creatures that makes you the entity you are."

"Each part we see—the trees, the grass, the road itself—are all just appendages to one giant creature?" asked Lorritson, showing the first sign of curiosity since leaving the thorny prison.

"Integral parts. No single one is vital, but all are necessary. It is difficult to conceive of all living things on a planet being aspects of the same creature, but I believe it is true here. If such is the case, the fission plant is likely to be organic in nature also."

"Organic fission isn't the same as nuclear fission." McCoy smirked.

"I am aware of that. And, Doctor, you must be aware of naturally occurring nuclear reactors. One became critical and ran for hundreds of years on your Earth, on the continent of Africa. Pitchblende in an underground vein proved rich enough to trigger fission. The rock of the continent itself contained the reaction. I contend such is the case here also."

"So the energy is used directly by the life form? There won't be turbines and other mechanical gadgets?"

"None," Spock answered his captain.

"Scotty'd be disappointed."

They walked to the top of a rise. Kirk spotted the facility first. Even as Spock had detailed, the fission reactor proved entirely organic, contained by huge, throbbing slabs of gray material that might have been animal muscle tissue.

"Those bands of gray hold inorganic shields in place. The heat within the core of the natural reactor builds. Some creature, possibly designed or evolved for the task, absorbs the heat directly and conducts it to the life form outside the radiation area."

"Nothing can live within an atomic pile, Spock," protested McCoy.

"Doctor, your biological education is curiously stunted. Do you not attempt to examine all the peculiar forms of life that exist within the bounds of our universe? Many forms of bacteria not only thrive within boiling water, they flourish also in the high-radiation environment of an atomic reactor."

"Never heard of any such critter."

"They exist and have been known for centuries. They were well documented even in the twentieth century."

"Captain," shouted one of the security men. "Look. There."

Kirk saw the shuttle roaring off from a quarry on the far side of the natural atomic reactor. The shuttle strained as it took to the air, trembling under the heavy load it carried. Without further discussion, Kirk motioned for the party to follow. If they hurried, they might arrive at the quarry site just before sundown.

* * *

"Everything is as I surmised, Captain," said Spock, his voice low. "Note how they all keep their communicators constantly linked with the *Enterprise*."

Kirk nodded. At times, he heard Lorelei's voice. The volume on all the communicators in the hands of his hypnotized crew had been turned to maximum. While they were some distance away, he felt the tuggings as Lorelei spoke her persuasive words. Peace. Nonaggression. The True Path.

Spock shook him out of his stupor. "Captain, if you concentrate too much, she will ensorcell you with her words—with her subsonics."

"I think you're right, Spock. There's no other reason for her to maintain such close verbal contact with the ground crew."

"The shielding is being mined by worms, sir," came one of the security men's report. "Giant worms with immense slasher mandibles. They cut through the rock just like they used atomic torches. Low-slung lizard creatures cart the cut slabs to the landing site, where we use antigrav lifters on it to get it into the shuttle. Where *they* use lifters," he corrected, tenseness in his voice.

"Relax, Mr. Neal, we're not going to have to fight our crew. There's got to be a better way."

"Thanks, sir. I . . . I don't like the idea of having to hurt any of them."

"Jim?" asked McCoy, fingers cutting into his arm. The doctor stared at the security officer.

"No, it's just his natural reluctance to harm his friends. I don't care for it, either. Lorelei hasn't got to him." In a lower voice he added, "And I'll see to it that she doesn't."

They observed for some time while the last of the shielding was loaded. The shuttle again roared aloft, leaving behind a handful of crewmen. One of them placed his

# Chapter Nine

*Captain's Log,* Stardate 4906.1

> We have secured a position on a hill overlooking the quarry where shielding for repair of the *Enterprise*'s engines is being mined. Tension mounts with each shuttleload of the shielding. There cannot be many more trips; the shuttle provides the only means of escaping this planet. Spock is unsure how much longer our presence will go undetected. As soon as the drug wears off on the thorny corral bush where he, McCoy and the others were imprisoned, the entire planet will be in an uproar. Escape must come soon—or we will never leave this planet alive.

"I estimate three point seven nine six two metric tons of shielding will give Mr. Scott adequate radiation protection.

That means there will be only one more trip of the shuttle."

"Why didn't they just beam it up?" asked McCoy. "It's time-consuming to come and pick it up like they're doing. Would it have angered the planetary life form?"

"Even disregarding the problem with the transporter's range-finder unit, Doctor, the sheer mass of shielding is too great to be beamed up. We are not talking about grams. Mr. Scott needed thousands of kilograms of mass to protect his workers as they repair the warp engines."

Silence fell. Shivers ran up and down Kirk's spine. The utter solitude of the spot wore on his nerves. No crickets chirped, no birds sang, no animal sounds at all penetrated to their hideout, because there were no such sounds anywhere on the planet. All performed as a single unit.

"When do you estimate the thornbush will begin throwing off the effects of the drug?"

Spock looked toward McCoy, who sat sullen and withdrawn. "The metabolism of the bush is unknown, but it cannot be longer than a few more hours. When that occurs, we will become the hunted once again."

"It's going to be cutting it close, no matter what. The last shuttle trip, the planet becoming aware of your absence, trying not to draw attention to ourselves until then." Kirk heaved a deep sigh. "And then our problems will only be starting. Regaining control of the *Enterprise* won't be an easy job."

"Lorelei has effectively bound all of the crew to her with the sonic hypnosis."

"It must go deeper than that, Spock," mused Kirk. "Just seeing her, I feel . . . different."

"It might not be a matter of sight as much as scent, in your case. She is of a different race, but her species pheromones might excite certain humans."

"Such as myself?" Kirk asked, smiling slightly. "It's possible. I did notice her perfume once. Thinking back, how could she have had any perfume? She didn't bring anything but the clothing she wore when we rescued her from the derelict."

"The planet Hyla will make an interesting and most valuable addition to the Federation if we can find it for contact."

"'If,' Spock? You're not turning into a pessimist, are you?"

"I only state such matters in a statistical sense. The odds against our successfully escaping this planet are—"

Kirk held up his hand and cut off his science officer's answer. "That's all right. You don't need to be specific. We all know there's not much hope."

"Hope, Captain? A purely human concept and one that does not sustain close analysis. It, like your bizarre idea of luck, actually refers to statistical concepts."

"Enough of this. Let's go over the plan one last time for getting on board the shuttle. Nothing can go wrong."

"Sir, many things can go wrong. If—"

"Spock, shut up," said McCoy. "I'm tired of you mouthing off all the time. I want to do something about it." He rose and started toward the Vulcan. As the doctor stepped out, his foot hit a stump. The seemingly dead tree recoiled and roots began rising from the soil, curling in toward the central stalk.

"Doctor, careful," cautioned Spock, pointing. "All is interconnected. Tread softly."

"Damnedest place I ever saw. Even the earthworms complain if you stomp too hard on the ground." He started to step down firmly, then hesitated. He gingerly walked the short distance and crouched beside Kirk and Spock. "All right. I'm learning. Can't knock out the entire planet, so I have to be careful."

"We won't be able to rush the shuttle. We dare not take the chance of alerting the planetary life form that anything is amiss. On the other hand, we can't just walk up without being spotted. There are guards posted while the actual loading is going on."

"We have hand phasers. Why not stun the guards, then take our sweet time waltzing over?" McCoy scratched his head and rocked back on his heels as they huddled together.

"Alerting the life form is only part of our concern. If Lorelei gets even a hint that her shuttle has been hijacked, she won't open the landing-bay doors. Or worse, she will leave orbit and find another planet to perform repairs. In either case, we are marooned."

"She has to believe everything is proceeding according to her plans," agreed Kirk, hating the mention of any part of the *Enterprise* as being "hers." We can take out the guards one by one and substitute our own men. But whoever is in command must remain so, because Lorelei will check frequently."

"This is becoming more complicated than the strategy for the battle at Rift Twenty-three when the Romulans tried to drive a wedge through the center of the Federation."

"Bones, our success or failure might reflect on history. That sounds like this is being blown out of proportion, but it isn't. Zarv and Lorritson still have a mission to perform. The Romulans aren't going to wait for us. The Ammdon-Jurnamoria spate will be escalated into a full war without peaceful alternatives."

"The shuttle, sir!" called one of the security team.

The distant roar provided a touch with a civilization totally different from the organic entity all around—and wonderfully familiar. A pair of the living airplanes silently flew above, as if they escorted the rapidly falling shuttle. When the shuttle banked and came in for a precision landing, the planetary life form's aerial watchdogs soared off on some other mission.

"This is it. Mr. Neal, take the guard on that rise. Spock, McCoy, stick close. The rest of you, wait here. Come only if we run into trouble." Kirk wanted as few involved as possible in the seizure of the shuttle. Too many hands and feet only added to the chance for mistake. The initial attack was the only chance they got. Flub it, and everything was lost.

Kirk watched the security man slip off, watching where every foot was placed. By the time the shuttle door opened and the crew emerged, Neal hid only a few meters away. They held their breath as the crewman from the shuttle marched past Neal's hiding spot. An eruption of red, a quick blow, a body slumping unconscious, and Neal replaced the guard. Kirk gave the high sign. The trio moved.

They cautiously passed down a small rise and waited while the willing workers dragged huge slabs of the rock shielding material up the hill to where the shuttle crew slid antigrav sleds beneath it.

"We can take the crew out, replace them and then get into the shuttle," said Kirk. "There doesn't seem to be any way of making a frontal assault on the shuttle."

"Sir, Mr. Scott is in command." Spock peered through the gathering twilight, his sharper eyes taking in more details than either Kirk or McCoy. "He will recognize us instantly if we attempt it."

"We don't have much other chance."

Spock shrugged. Whether he agreed or not, his captain had made a command decision. They were all bound by it now.

"Now!"

The trio surged up from their hiding spots and tackled the workers jockeying the antigrav sleds into place under the slabs of shielding. Kirk hit his man twice before knocking him out. Spock's fingers tightened on a collarbone in a Vulcan nerve pinch. Only McCoy had trouble subduing his man; all the while he grunted and grumbled about doctors helping and not harming their patients.

"In this case, Doctor," said Spock, "it is all too apparent he is your victim rather than your patient."

"You're right, Spock. He's my victim. And for pointing it out to me, I'll give you a free cosmetic ear job when I get back to my surgery. Might make you more human, though I doubt it."

"Such does not appeal to me in the least, Dr. McCoy."

Kirk motioned for them to finish the job the others had begun. They positioned the antigrav sleds and began tugging them along toward the shuttle some distance away. The creatures that had been dragging the slabs of shielding paid them no more attention than they had the other humans. To them, one extraneous creature was identical to another—as long as they/it was not threatened.

"Easy does it," said Kirk, more to McCoy than to Spock. "Don't even give a hint that anything's wrong."

"There's Scotty," whispered McCoy. "He's looking the other way."

"Into the shuttle's hold. Then we can see about him."

They guided the heavy shielding into the shuttle hold, secured the load with force bands and sent the antigrav sleds back out into the gathering darkness. The twin-bladed sleds hovered quietly, obediently waiting for the next trip to the quarry. If Kirk had his way, that trip would be delayed.

"All right," he said, pressing close to the side of the shuttle. "We've got to do this all in one quick attack. Spock, you take out Scotty with your nerve pinch. Bones and I will go after the others inside the shuttle."

"How will we get inside in time to do anything? They'll be able to warn Lorelei."

"Confidence, Bones. Set? Go!"

The trio slipped free of the hold and started for their targets when a loud warning shout echoed up the path from the direction of the quarry. The cry was wordless, anguished—and human.

"Lads," ordered Scotty, moving around from his position near the front of the shuttle. "Go and see what trouble's brewin' down there. I dinna like this place." As two of the security team with him trotted off, phasers still holstered, Scotty flipped open his communicator. "Come in, *Enterprise*."

Response came instantly.

"What trouble, Mr. Scott?" sounded Lorelei's dulcet tones. "There hasn't been any intervention with the planet's biosphere?"

"I kenna the problem, Lorelei." As Scotty continued speaking, Kirk waved back both his friends. Even at five meters and over a small hand communicator, the hypnotic effect of the Hylan woman's voice made itself felt.

Kirk motioned for the others to put hands over ears. They duplicated his action while hiding in the cargo hold once more. Spock occasionally peered around the corner, checking to be certain Scotty still spoke into the communicator. He whirled back to face the others. His lips moved in silent confirmation that contact between Lorelei and the ground remained active.

Kirk moved close to Spock and whispered in his ear, "Let's get back down the trail and find out what happened. We can't leave Zarv and the others if they were discovered."

Spock and McCoy grabbed the handholds on the sides

of the antigrav sleds and pushed them back down the path toward the quarry, as if they carried on with their assignment. The cloak of darkness now hid them from Scotty's eyes. They were only ebony forms moving through the night.

At a safe distance, Kirk spoke aloud. "Do either of you see anything? Someone cried out. It had to be one of our men."

"Not necessarily, Captain. If the man Neal took out or even one of those you or Dr. McCoy struck regained consciousness, he might have inadvertently lashed out and angered the planetary life form. If such is the case, we have very few minutes left."

Kirk didn't want to consider the other possibility. The drug injected into the thornbush might have worn off. If so, the entire planet might be seeking its escaped prisoners. No matter what had happened, the planet had been disturbed.

"There. Look!"

The two security men Scotty had dispatched to check out the quarry were trapped next to a large boulder. At their feet snapped knee-high four-legged animals with fangs long enough to cut through two inches of solid wood. The loud snapping noises as jaws opened and closed indicated the animals meant harm.

"No phasers," cautioned Kirk as McCoy drew his. "That's what caused this mess. See?" He pointed to several of the predator animals lying stunned near the three humans they had knocked out earlier. The men's throats had been ripped out.

"So much for your Vulcan nerve pinch. You put him out too good, Spock. The dogs got him."

"This planet's ecosystem is precise. The scavengers—and that is what those beasts must be—found those we disabled. When those we rendered unconscious didn't stir or respond in an approved fashion, they began their function."

"They were eating them!"

"The creatures were removing potentially rotting meat. None of those we disabled reported in to the master life form; therefore it became obvious that function had terminated."

Kirk restrained McCoy again as the doctor raised a phaser.

"Let me stop them, Jim. If we don't do something, those men will die. Whether or not they're bewitched by Lorelei, they're still crewmen from the *Enterprise*. *Your* ship."

"Bones." James T. Kirk felt the dilemma pulling him apart. If they acted swiftly, they might prevent the deaths of the other two men. But if Kirk or either of the others with him did act, it would not only alert and alarm the planetary life form, it would reveal their presence to Scotty— and Lorelei. Escape would never be possible.

If they did nothing, two of his crew died. *His* crew.

"Jim, what are you going to do?" demanded McCoy. "They can't hold off the creatures much longer."

"They do not use their phasers. Lorelei's pacifistic philosophy has been too deeply ingrained for them to even defend their own lives. Fascinating, if evolutionally maladaptive."

"Scott, help!" Kirk bellowed. He pulled his two friends aside, away from the path, into shadows too deep for anyone to see them.

Seconds later, Montgomery Scott lumbered down the trail.

"Saints preserve us, they're bein' eaten alive!" He spoke directly into the communicator.

"Peace!" came Lorelei's voice. The word rolled out,

soothed, diminished the feverish snapping activity of the animals—the multiple extensions of the planetary life. "These men meant no harm. They live. They react. Do not harm them. They are one with the others."

Kirk held his hands firmly over his ears to block out Lorelei's words. Even that did not prevent the full impact of her sonic suasions. But enough filtered out so that he maintained his own ideals, his own philosophies. Lorelei spoke for fifteen minutes, coaxing, cajoling, soothing. The end result was all that Kirk might have hoped.

The pack of scavenger animals snuffled about, reluctant, then left to pursue their function elsewhere. The two rescued men clung to each other for support. Shock and their wounds prevented them from doing much more than shaking. The sight of their three friends, all bloody and dead, unnerved them even more. Scotty motioned for them to return to the shuttle. Kirk watched and waited, wondering what opportunity this might provide. His crew was being decimated; every loss for those obeying Lorelei wasn't a victory. Those were *his* men dying.

When Scotty finished his report and closed the communicator lid, he shook his head and moved to put the bodies onto one of the antigrav sleds Spock had left at the edge of the path. Mumbling to himself, the engineer pushed the grisly load back to the shuttle.

"He'll call it quits," warned McCoy. "With so many men dead, he'll want to return to the *Enterprise*. There can't be any further need for shielding. They've got enough."

"You're right, Bones. This is the flare-off. Go get Neal and the others. Approach slowly. Spock and I will try to take out Scotty. This is our best chance."

"It's our only chance."

Kirk didn't answer the doctor. He waited until McCoy had slipped off into the night, carefully walking to avoid any chance of disturbing the touchy organism forming the ecosphere around them. Kirk took a deep breath, then set off for the shuttle. The time had come to act. If they didn't get into the shuttle soon, it'd leave and strand them forever on the planet. He doubted if Lorelei or any of the others aboard the *Enterprise* wanted to return after this bloody disaster.

"There, Jim. He is closing the cargo hatch."

Kirk nodded, waited for Spock to move quietly toward Scotty, then stood and walked into an area illuminated by a small hand torch placed near the hatch of the shuttle. He stopped, hands on hips, and stood watching Scotty.

The engineer did a double take.

"Captain, 'tis you!" Then his expression shifted from joy to outrage. "Ye shouldn't hae come like this. Lorelei says ye are exiled. Ye are a disruptive influence."

"I need to return to my ship, Scotty. Let me return on the shuttle." Kirk turned and patted the cold metal hull. "The old *Galileo Seven* has had a checkered career, hasn't it?"

"Captain, I canna make ye leave, but Lorelei is a persuasive lass." Scotty reached for the communicator. He froze, muscles tensed, as Spock used the Vulcan nerve pinch to stop him.

"I wondered if you'd forgotten what you were supposed to do."

One eyebrow arched. "Captain," said Spock, "I did not forget. There are beasts afoot in the dark. I did not wish to disturb them."

"Get on with it, Spock," Kirk said, a feeling of unease growing. "Have you ever heard the expression, 'Someone is walking on my grave'? I'm getting that sensation now." He looked out into the dark. Seeing nothing, he hefted the hand torch and flashed it around. Bootheels crunching against gravel sounded. McCoy, Neal and the others entered the yellow cone of light. Ambassador Zarv and Donald Lorritson trailed behind, still cowed from their experiences.

"We've got to work on Scotty before getting back to the *Enterprise,*" he explained. "There are still a couple inside who haven't, uh, seen the error of their ways."

"Here's one who is still pretty mad about it all, Captain." Neal dumped down the guard he'd slugged. The man struggled in the tight bonds fastening wrists and ankles. A thick section of tunic muffled his protests.

"Keep it all quiet. Spock, what do you think?"

"Mr. Scott is not likely to throw off the effects of Lorelei's sonic brainwashing easily if this man is any example of her effectiveness." He pointed to the struggling security guard. "He has been removed from her sonic persuasions for some twenty minutes and still persists."

"Does it have to be?" asked McCoy. "Do you have to do it to Scotty?"

"I see no alternative."

Kirk nodded brusquely. "Do it, Spock. Use the Vulcan mind fusion. Try to convince him that he must aid us."

"Even if Spock succeeds, we're all still vulnerable if we come within her hearing," protested Neal.

"Doctor, do you think you can work up a suitable replacement for ear wax?"

McCoy smiled and said, "It worked just fine for Odysseus. No Siren is going to bother us when I'm finished. Neal, help me search through the cargo hold. I'm needing a ball of jeweler's wax kept back there for taking impressions." McCoy and the security guard hurried off.

Jim Kirk turned and watched Spock reaching out, fingers caressing Scotty's face. The fingers stiffened, probing firmly. Both Spock and Scott jerked, the Vulcan's face turning flaccid.

"He is . . . his mind is awash with conflict," came a voice subtly different from Spock's, yet one obviously belonging to the Vulcan. "I cannot order it all. The words—her words—confuse and addle and create turmoil. So close. So close to finding the equation to free myself. Himself." Spock pulled away as if his hands had been burned by the engineer's flesh.

"Spock, are you all right?"

"Eminently so, Captain. I believe I have succeeded, at least in part."

"Captain Kirk, I remember it now. I tried to stop ye. Gods, how can I hold my head up after this?" The man put his head down into his cupped hands and shook all over. "Never have I disgraced myself like this. 'Tis a tragedy."

"It'll be a tragedy if we don't get out of here. You're able to help us, Scotty?"

"Aye, Captain. Anything. To . . . the *Enterprise*. She has control of the *Enterprise*. Lorelei!"

"It will come back slowly. I neurologically rearranged certain pathways. He will not be harmed, but his memory will be chaotic for some days."

"Mr. Spock, it was you who was a-foolin' about in my head!"

Kirk looked up to see McCoy and Neal returning. McCoy smiled, holding aloft a large ball of the soft, pliant wax.

"Here's our ticket back to Mount Olympus."

"Please, Doctor, your classical allusions fall on deaf ears."

Leonard McCoy stopped and stared, mouth open. "If I didn't know better, I'd think Spock had made a joke."

"Later, Bones. Will this really work?"

"It'll have to. It's all I could find. Cram it in good. There. I'll irrigate your aural channels later and clean out the mess." He went from one to another in the group until all ears were plugged. Satisfied, he helped Neal get their prisoner into the shuttle hold. It took even less time to capture the two who had been beset by the scavengers. They put up no fight, their spirits already low. With some satisfaction, McCoy oversaw them being tied and gagged. With no further influence of Lorelei over the men, the security guards would return to normal in a few hours—or days. Till then they had to remain tied. Spock's services couldn't be spared for each in the party. Not at this crucial moment.

"Into the shuttle. I want off this planet as soon as possible. There's a feeling of impending disaster I can't shake."

"Captain Kirk," said Lorritson, "I have misjudged you. This has been a trying time for all of us. You handled yourself admirably."

"Inside. We can pat each other on the back later. When we've retaken the *Enterprise* from Lorelei." Kirk waved Ambassador Zarv in, then noticed the Tellarite standing frozen in place just outside the shuttle hatch. "Ambassador!" he shouted, wanting to penetrate the veil dropped by the wax in their ears.

"Zarv! No, you can't!" screamed Lorritson. Before anyone could stop him, Donald Lorritson rocketed from the shuttle and rushed to his superior's side. The Tellarite's leg had become wrapped in a strong vine. Others sprouted out of the soil and worked forward, groping blindly for the ambassador.

"Spock, hold off," he ordered. "Zarv's caught by vines."

"The planetary life form is now aware of our escape, Jim. The shuttle sensors report accelerated activity throughout the immediate area. Fliers are aloft and armies of humanoids approach from the direction of the city. We have no time left. None!"

"I've got to save him. Without them, there won't be an Ammdon peace mission."

Kirk hurled out the open hatchway, crushed down viciously on a vine working its way through the dirt and kicked free to stand beside Lorritson. The man shook as if he had a palsy. It took only a glance to see what produced this reaction. A vine had circled Zarv's throat and choked the Tellarite to death. His tongue hung from his piglike snout, purple and bloated. His beady eyes had bulged to the point where the grotesque sight turned Kirk's stomach.

"Donald, back. You can't help him now. You're the ambassador. You'll have to stop the Ammdon-Jurnamoria war."

"Zarv," he sobbed. "He was more than my superior. He . . . he was my friend. It's so hard to believe. We complemented each other so well. We were invincible as a negotiating team. And with Mek Jokkor—"

"Lorritson! Snap to it!" Kirk lashed out with his boots, trying to clear a path to the shuttle. There wasn't any chance. He whipped out his phaser. Two quick rayings produced results, but not what Kirk had expected.

The vines recoiled and shriveled, sinking back into the soil. But response came from all other quarters. A furred leg batted thc weapon from his grip. Tendrils snaked up to grip his legs. Lorritson already flopped about on hands and knees, unable to stand. Kirk fought, but to no avail. The force of an entire planet weighed against him.

"Spock!" he screamed. "Take off. Leave me. Get the *Enterprise* back. Stop Lorelei!"

His stoppered ears did not permit him to hear the exchange between Spock and McCoy. He saw his science officer shove McCoy back, then slam down the hatch. An odd combination of pride and fear racked him. Spock had sense enough to obey. The *Enterprise* would be retaken. But abandonment now meant death.

The shuttle engines flared into life. Hot exhaust gases lashed his face, his hands, his entire body.

But the *Galileo Seven* did not blast off. Spock turned the shuttle so that the engine-igniter flames continued to spew backward. Kirk fought even harder when he realized what Spock was doing. He still had a chance to escape. The heat caused the life form assailing him to wither, to loosen its grip. He kicked away vines, shoved off groping hands, struggled forward into the teeth of the blast.

"Hurry, Captain. I cannot hold this much longer." The words came muffled and indistinct, but he knew. He jerked free of the last vine holding him and rushed for the shuttle hatch. Strong hands pulled him inside.

"Zarv, Lorritson, both died," he managed to say.

"You're alive," he heard someone shout.

Then, as the shuttle engines flared to full-throated life and the pressure of intense acceleration slammed him into steel deck plates, Jim Kirk passed out. His last thoughts were of death and . . . Lorelei.

# Chapter Ten

*Captain's Log,* Stardate 4908.0

> It is hard to believe that escape from the uni-life planetary system might be the easiest part of regaining control of the *Enterprise*. Lorelei's hold on the crew is as sure as if she had them chained—surer. The silver curtain of her words has woven them into a bind that will take time and effort to correct. We have no time left.

"Be careful, Spock. You're getting too close."

"Doctor, I am a qualified pilot. I need not be warned of such elementary concerns. Please tend to your patients. I can only hope that your medical skills surpass your piloting abilities."

"As you were," snapped Kirk, forcing himself to sit upright. He remembered passing out on the steel deck plates. He now rested in one of the padded acceleration couches. He had no memory of being lifted and strapped in. "Report."

"Sir, we are less than a thousand meters from the *Enterprise*. Mr. Scott has contacted those in the landing bay. The bay doors are opening in response. We will soon be berthed."

"Aye, Captain. Look. The repairs are goin' accordin' to plan." Scotty pushed past his captain to point through the tiny windows. "The shieldin's in place and they canna work faster. Bonny lads and lasses." He beamed in pleasure at the sight of the matter-antimatter pods being reconstructed so expertly. One entire warp engine had been stripped and repaired. The shielding hovered just millimeters from the deadly antimatter, held in place by invisible force fields. When finished, the magnetic bottles would be re-formed and the potent power source for the starship reignited.

"We've got seven men able to withstand Lorelei's voice. Will it be enough?" Kirk wondered out loud.

"I have considered this point, Captain. If we stun those in the landing bay, we can gain immediate entry to the engineering levels. From there, it is simple enough to trigger the sleep-gas canisters. While it is an inconvenience to allow four hundred and twenty-three of the crew to so abandon their duties simultaneously, it is better than attempting a piecemeal conquest."

"As usual, Spock, your analysis is masterful." Kirk sighed. "I wish it were possible to do it that way. Lorelei has had free run of the ship. She's probably disconnected the sleep-gas canisters."

"It is a peaceful device, Captain. Is that not the basis for her philosophy?"

"It can be turned against her. Her takeover wasn't immediate. It wouldn't surprise me in the least to find that most of the internal defense devices have been deactivated."

"Even if they were workin'," said Scotty, "many of the crew are outside. The least squawk, and an entire engineerin' team will be down on you."

"They can't physically oppose us if they believe in pacifism," burst in Mr. Neal. "That's something we have over them. We can fight and they can't."

"They're still friends and crewmates, mister," Kirk said sharply. "And pacifism doesn't mean they can't imprison us for our own good. They outnumber us sixty to one. Our only advantage is surprise."

"And speed. We can move quick if we have to."

"Aye, speed. Surprise," agreed Scotty. "But if you're thinkin' the sleepy gas is nae gonna work, what are we to do?"

"We take Lorelei prisoner. Hold her in an isolation detention cell and prevent her from contacting any of the others. If the sleep gas works, fine. If not, her sonic influence will decrease."

"It will be an exponential decrease," said Spock. "The first few days will show the most rapid decline in influence; then it will tail off. When we return to starbase, it might be required that a full psychological profile be worked for each crew member."

"Except yourself, of course," said McCoy. "You Vulcans are impervious to her charms, I take it?"

"I detect only small influences on my own behavior. Unlike humans, we are able to logically cross-check our actions. Now, Doctor, if you will excuse me for a moment, I must dock this craft."

Ahead, bay doors yawned wide. Spock expertly guided them through and touched down with the slightest of shocks. He glanced at Kirk, who stood shakily, regaining his equilibrium after the blow to his head. In his hand he clutched a phaser, set on stun.

"Let's go. Lorelei will probably be on the bridge. Phaser-stun as many as you can, don't allow anyone to escape and spread the alarm, and I'll see you when we're in charge again."

"Good luck, Captain." Spock solemnly nodded, then clutched Kirk's shoulder.

James T. Kirk turned and signaled Neal to open the hatch. Even before the hatch had risen all the way, Kirk sent a flashing red beam of phaser fire through the opening. Two landing-bay technicians slumped, unconscious. The marauders piled out, firing quickly at unsuspecting targets.

Finally Scotty said, "There's the lot, Captain. Let me report in to the wee lass on the bridge." He flipped open his communicator and said, "Lorelei, this is Scott reportin' a successful return. The last of the shieldin' is bein' unloaded now."

"Very good, Mr. Scott. You have done well." Kirk watched as the expression on Scotty's face altered slightly. Even with the wax plugging his ears, he heard enough of the alien woman's beguiling words to feel the tug back toward servitude. Kirk reached out and shook his engineer. Scotty blinked and quickly nodded. He wouldn't succumb easily. Not again.

At a dead run, they reached the turboelevator and crowded within. The wax robbed them of the usual sounds, the whishing past floors, the electronic hums, the soft grating of metal on metal as the door opened onto the bridge. Kirk took two quick steps forward.

Lorelei sat in his command seat, attention focused on the viewscreen. Kirk's gaze flickered from the woman to the picture of his crew diligently working on engine repair, then returned. In that fraction of a second, Lorelei had sensed the intrusion and hit the alarm button. Red lights flared and the general-quarters warning flashed on and off.

Spock and Kirk began firing their phasers. Chekov and Sulu slumped forward, stunned. Uhura tried to interpose her body between the beams and Lorelei's slim body. She succeeded in taking a double blast. All the while, Lorelei moved quickly to the emergency stairs leading to the deck below.

Air blew against Kirk's back. He spun, to face the closed doors to the turbolift. McCoy and Neal had gone down, to try to head off the Hylan. The others on the deck rushed forward, only to be stunned by Spock's accurate fire. In less than fifteen seconds, all lay peacefully dozing.

"Damn, Spock, she got away from us."

"We have control of the ship, Captain. The bridge is vital if she wants to regain power."

Kirk dropped into his seat, flipped a code on the buttons and waited. No red lights blossomed on Chekov's panel.

"She deactivated the gas canisters, as I thought she might. We may have the bridge, but she has the rest of the ship. By the time she reaches auxiliary control, we're going to have a problem on our hands."

"The turbolift is now disabled. The only way to reach the bridge is up the stairwell."

"Or through the dome." Kirk looked up at the glasteel skylight magnifying the stars. An atomic torch might cut through it in a few minutes. They'd have warning, but it'd avail them little. The sudden decompression would kill them. He tried to force from his mind the thought of the engineering team working on the dome rather than the warp drive. His frontal attack had almost succeeded.

A near miss—and in this case, a millimeter might as well have been a parsec. Lorelei had escaped unscathed, in full control of the crew and able to bide her time. For Kirk and the others, time worked as their enemy.

"Sir, I have Mr. Scott on the intercom."

"Report, Scotty."

"I have secured a portion of the engine room. Heather McConel is likely to be back in full form soon enough. The lass seldom washed her ears." He chuckled at this. "The others, now, they'll pose a wee problem. I have them locked in a tool bin."

"Weld the door shut. And weld shut the door leading into the engineering section. We didn't get Lorelei. She will have the rest of the crew down on our necks any minute now. The best we can do is slow her down."

"Aye, aye, sair."

Scotty clicked off, leaving Kirk to his bleak thoughts. The hum of Spock's phaser pulled him back. Three crewmen collapsed at the head of the stairs. When the turbolift doors opened, Kirk was ready. His phaser stunned six inside. The doors closed and the elevator dropped back.

"I thought you had the turboelevator shut down."

"Sorry, Captain. Lorlei has established herself in the auxiliary command post. She overrode me."

"Is there any part of the ship you have total control over?"

"Negative, sir. Mr. Scott might allow me some slight control, but with the warp engines still powered down and most internal energy coming from batteries and impulse power, there is not a great deal we can do."

"Shut off the air-circulating fans. We were only running them at fifty percent."

"Lorelei has overriden control already. We cannot affect any of the life-support units. Nor can I overload by switching in other power-draining equipment."

"Keep trying. We can't give it up now. We can't."

Even as he spoke, the viewscreen blurred and the repair crew vanished, to be replaced by Lorelei's sad face.

"James? It is truly you. You are a most remarkable man. It is a pity you so steadfastly refuse to forsake the ways of violence."

Kirk swallowed hard. Even the sight of the woman affected him. Pheromones, harmonics, more? He didn't know. The wax filtered out the worst of her persuasive tones, but he still shivered at the impact of her words.

"Filter her down even more, can you, Spock?"

"At once, Captain."

The picture remained, but herringbone patterns crisscrossed her visage now. The words came slurred and indistinct, but Kirk still understood them all too well.

"You cannot escape or triumph. Please surrender, James. I do not wish to see you come to any harm." When he did not respond, she smiled sadly and added, "Your Dr. McCoy has been captured."

"Bones!" Kirk half-rose, hands on the armrests, poised to explode outward.

"He will be beamed back to the planet. I will try to explain to the being comprising that planet of the situation. No disciplinary action will be taken against McCoy. He must only learn to live in harmony with the ecosystem."

"You'll kill him. None of us can live there. We're intruders. That's a totally symbiotic system!"

"I have the screen set for mark two filter, Captain. She can neither see nor hear you clearly."

"She's got McCoy." He sank back into his seat, suddenly weary to the core of his soul.

"James, please do not react in so violent a fashion." Kirk repeatedly rammed his fists into the armrests of his command seat. He trembled with the need to act, to do something—and the frustration of being totally helpless. "Dr. McCoy is not being harmed. If anything, he is better off now than when you sneaked back aboard. Many minor injuries have been tended to. Nurse Chapel is quite able to handle such wounds as the doctor sported."

"Lorelei, you're going to beam him back down to the planet."

"I cannot have dissension among the crew. Violence is a seed spawning nothing but more violence. I tried to reason with you and failed. McCoy is similarly committed to a course at odds with the True Path."

"He'll die on the planet. The ecosystem is—"

"I am aware of the unified order of life on the planet," the woman broke in. Kirk felt the vibrancy of her voice, the light she brought to an otherwise darkened universe. She promised so much. Why did he oppose her so? Peace was his for the asking. All he had to do was to listen, to listen, to listen.

"Captain," shouted Spock, breaking the spell the Hylan wove around him. "It is not wise conversing with her for even short periods of time."

Jim Kirk shook himself. The wax in their ears did not do more than take the edge off the woman's harmonic attacks. She pitched her voice perfectly, insidiously. But he resisted, knowing what weapon he faced. A weapon was the only way he could consider her voice.

It didn't matter that what Lorelei preached—and truly believed, he was certain—was peace. That philosophy would cause any human to die quickly on the planet below. Kirk wondered if Lorelei herself could survive in the uni-life-form system. It transcended symbiosis; it became one huge organism living and responding as a unit. Anyone—human, Hylan, Tellarite—that intervened became a cancer to be removed before the system suffered. It was a potent evolutionary development, and one Kirk wished he and his crew had time to study further—at their leisure and in such a way that the life form did not view them as intruders.

"Lorelei, don't send McCoy back down to the planet. He doesn't belong there."

"He no longer fits in aboard the *Enterprise*, either, James. Nor do you. In the scheme of things, the old order must make way for the new. You are not adaptive enough to embrace the ways of peace. The ways of war are no longer needed."

"Lorelei," he started, then switched off the viewscreen. An exterior view of the repair work being finished on the port engine replaced the woman's drawn face.

"This is quite a strain on her," he told Spock. "Do you see the sadness in her eyes, the way she looks?"

"Undoubtedly it is a strain, Captain. She cannot like what she does in the name of peace. Any being proclaiming allegiance to pacifism knows the planet below will slay. She is only offering a tenuous chance to survive."

"It is an effort," mused Kirk.

"No, Jim, that won't be good enough to defeat her. She conserves her personal strength well."

"I can't let her send McCoy down. I'll stop her. Spock, keep trying to box her in with the controls. I'll try to rescue McCoy in the transporter."

"Sir, I have an idea that might work. It requires considerable computer work on my part, however."

"Get me down to the transporter room; then do what you have to."

"Aye, aye, sir. Ready."

The doors to the turbolift slipped open. Kirk walked forward as if he marched into the maw of a giant beast preparing to devour him. Never had he felt more alone than when the doors slid shut and the elevator dropped at breathtaking speed. Kirk had barely steeled himself for the hostile reception committee waiting as the doors opened on the transporter deck.

Swift reflexes saved him. Half a dozen members of a security team bracketed the hall, phasers set on stun. His own phaser fired first, slid along the line of waiting guards and dropped them in one efficient motion. Lorelei controlled his crew, but their reflexes had yet to adapt to her words. They fought themselves, her enforced philosophy eventually triumphing. But the small delay between obedience to the Hylan and her pacifistic views and attacking a senior officer gave Kirk a slight edge.

The last of the security force had barely touched the deck when he burst into the transporter room. The transporter chief readied the unit and McCoy stood, hands bound behind his back.

"Off the plate, Bones," he yelled. "Deactivate transporter, Mr. Kyle." Again came the slight confusion, the merest of time lags. Kyle wanted to obey his captain; training so instilled died hard. But Lorelei had ordered him to beam down the doctor.

"Captain, I—" was all Kyle said before the phaser sent him reeling, to hit the wall and slide to the deck, unconscious.

"It's good to see you, Jim. You sure do cut it fine."

"Never mind that. We've got to get back to the bridge. Spock is trying to hold together what little control we have from there."

"How'd you get here? She took over from auxiliary." McCoy rubbed his wrists to get back the circulation that had been cut off due to the tightly fastened ropes.

"I . . . I don't know. Spock must have done it."

"No, James, I allowed it. Keeping you and the Vulcan

together did not seem a good tactic for me." Her voice boomed from the intercom near the transporter console.

"Tactic, Lorelei? You speak like a general. A military commander. Are you declaring war?" He motioned for McCoy to leave the room and head for the turbolift.

"War? That is not possible, according to your definition of war. In a way, it might be war, if you redefine it to mean convincing another of your moral superiority. Force solves nothing. We must all reason together peacefully. You are unable to do so. You resist too strongly."

"Jim, my ears. I . . . I feel her voice."

With the swiftness of striking lightning, Kirk moved. The flats of his hands slammed into either side of McCoy's head, trapping the man's ears in a quick slap. The doctor yelped and put his own hands over his injured ears.

"Dammit, you deafened me!" he shouted, no longer able to hear his own voice and control the volume. He subsided when Kirk put a finger to his lips, cautioning silence. McCoy realized then the need for such action.

"Still you persist in opposing my guidance to the True Path. I like you, James. I wish we had met under better circumstances. I must send you, too, to the planet. You disturb the crew with your savage ways."

The door leading from the transporter room slid shut. Kirk knew Lorelei had control restored over many of the circuits he'd shut down. He never hesitated when he slid the selector switch on the hand phaser to full power. The fuchsia beam lashed out against the door. A smoking hole widened until both men were able to slip through. Bits of burning metal caught on Kirk's tunic and smoldered through to naked flesh. He swatted them out, hardly noticing what he did as he ran for the stairs leading to the engineering section. If Scotty still held out, there was a slight chance he might be able to use this as a base to launch a frontal assault on the auxiliary bridge.

"No, James, it will not work. Do not harm any of the crew. They are your friends. They mean you no ill. Help them. Work together with them." He stumbled as he ran, the full force of her voice working on his resolve. In his head, he tried to recite poetry, to go over the crew roster, to think about anything but the softly persuasive tendrils drifting through his mind. Without the wax stoppers in his ears he'd have completely succumbed to Lorelei's expert ministrations.

"James, you want to believe as I do. Barbarism is not the answer. Friendship is. Working with others gives good feelings. There is more than . . ." Shrieking feedback cut through Kirk's mounting stupor like a knife through butter. The intercom went berserk with high-pitched whines, subsonic whirrings that rattled his bones and vibrated his internal organs. McCoy supported him until he got control of himself.

The shriekings of tormented electrons came as music to his ears. He could not make himself heard over it. He mouthed out, "To the auxiliary bridge." McCoy nodded and followed.

Kirk phaser-stunned two guards outside the door, then shoved through, ready to continue the fight. There was no need. Lorelei sat in the auxiliary command seat, her face haggard and drawn from effort. She spoke and the words amplified, fed on themselves and blasted forth as twisted gibberish.

"James," she said, the name screeching like a fingernail on metal finish. He shared her sadness and regret in that instant. His thumb tightened on the trigger and a pure beam of energy bathed the Hylan woman. She collapsed onto the control console. McCoy hurried to her side, checked her vital signs and nodded. She'd live.

So would the *Enterprise* and its crew.

Kirk went to the frail form and hoisted it in his arms. McCoy, phaser ready, trailed behind. No words were possible, even if the feedback from each activated intercom had allowed them.

James T. Kirk looked at the woman through the shimmer of a force curtain. Lorelei sat comfortably in the detention cell, unable to communicate with anyone on the outside. Kirk looked at his science officer. Spock nodded, saying, "The circuit is completed. It will work according to your specifications, Captain."

"Thank you, Spock." Kirk flipped the switch on a small black box. A single red light came on. "Are you able to hear me all right, Lorelei?"

"Yes, James," came the muted, frequency-altered reply. It sounded as if a basso profondo spoke and not the normal contralto that was Lorelei's. "You do not have to lock me up in this fashion."

"I'm sorry, Lorelei. I do. You threaten our mission. Only by keeping you isolated and in such a way that you can't use your . . ." He hesitated. He had started to say "weapon." ". . . so you can't use your persuasiveness against anyone on the ship can I ensure completion of our mission."

"You persist in going to Ammdon? A war will result."

"I don't believe that."

"The ambassadors are all dead. They were men of war, not peace. Their aggressions destroyed them."

"They died, but not from aggression. Humans are different. We don't fit the mold you tried to carve for us. Ambassador Zarv was a Tellarite. Not human, but enough like us. Mek Jokkor wasn't even vaguely human, except in exterior form, and he didn't fit into that planet's biosphere. Lorelei, it is difficult for you to accept, but there are places in the universe where humankind is not welcome, doesn't belong, will never belong."

"Peace is the answer."

"For the most part, you're right. It does not pay to pursue a warlike policy of expansion like the Klingons and the Romulans, but a peaceful society must be able to defend itself."

"Persuasion is enough."

"For Hyla, it might be. For humanity, it isn't." She gave him a pitying look, as if he'd missed the point entirely. He finally said, "I'll see that you're returned to Hyla as soon as possible."

"You will not kill me?"

"If you have to ask, *you've* missed the point." He flipped the switch on the black box and let the red light fade into darkness. Turning to Neal, he said, "See to it that no one else is allowed to communicate with her. The majority of the crew is still under her influence. According to McCoy's estimates, the effects will lessen over the next few days, with only lingering guilt by the end of a week. Till then, no chances. Right, Mr. Neal?"

"Aye, aye, sir." He saluted as Kirk and Spock left.

Once out in the corridor, Spock activated still another force barrier. Only then did he address Kirk. "Sir, Mr. Scott requests your immediate presence in engineering. His repair work has reached a crucial point."

"Very well. Carry on, Mr. Spock. Make certain that those with you on the bridge are absolutely loyal—to the Federation."

"Uhura, Sulu and Chekov are all cleared. I have used the Vulcan mind fusion to ascertain their true allegiances."

"Excellent." Kirk dropped down a stairway and worked his way through the confused jumbles of crew until he reached the engineering deck. The door had been pried open after Lorelei had been incarcerated. Repairing it might take as long as fixing the engines.

"Ah, Captain, I have something for ye to see." Scotty gestured for him to study the computer readouts.

"What is it? Hmm, here's the power level. Rising nicely. The port engine is fine. Good work."

"Captain, look at the starboard engine. The one we're workin' on now. The wee bairn's nae doin' so fine."

Needle-sharp power fluctuations confirmed Scotty's opinion. Kirk knew little about the details of the engines, but he'd trained long enough and had commanded a starship for enough years to recognize dangerous malfunctions when he spotted them. He looked up, frowning.

"Aye, sair, it's bad. I request pairmission to personally go out and dig about in the starboard matter-antimatter pod."

"There's no way you can use robot probes?"

"None, sair. 'Tis delicate work. Too delicate to trust to robotic waldoes."

"When you complete the matter-antimatter mixing balance the engine will run smoothly?"

"As smooth as a baby's bottom, sair!" he said proudly. Kirk had his answer. Scotty wanted his hands on the sensitive equipment in the pod, but he also had to do the work personally. None other had his talent, skill or experience.

"Do it. Keep the number of technicians accompanying you to a minimum. You know why."

"Their recovery from the wee lass's voiced brainwashing. Aye, sair. Uh, all the aid I'll be requirin' is Chief McConel." Kirk turned and sharply looked at the engineering chief. She stood to one side, chewing on her tongue as she adjusted part of the stabilizer circuit. "She's the best I've got, Captain."

"I know. Get on with it. And stay in contact with Spock. He might be able to suggest something if you have any troubles."

"Sair, what we have to do isn't hard. It's just dangerous."

"Well, Spock, how're they coming?" Kirk demanded. He bit down on his thumb as he watched the tiny spacesuited figures moving about on the starboard engine pod. "What's their status?"

"Matters have not materially changed since you asked three point two four minutes ago, Captain." Spock seemed impervious to the tension that sparked like electricity around the bridge.

"Dammit, this is important. They're in mortal danger out there."

"Yes, sir, they are."

McCoy snorted. "Don't pay him any mind, Jim. He's got cryogenic fluid running through his veins. They took out any human feelings and put in machinery."

"Doctor, all my parts are original. As to your implication that nonorganic parts are somehow inferior, allow me to recommend several competent papers on the topic."

"Quiet," snapped Kirk. "Report, Spock. How's Scotty doing?"

As if in answer, the engineer's voice crackled over the ship's intercom. "The magnetic bottle has been reestablished, but 'tis not the proper configuration. The MHD flow is constricted."

"What's that mean?" asked McCoy. "MHD's got something to do with the bottle?"

"It is the magnetohydrodynamic system that is out of

adjustment. Without perfect symmetry in the magnetic confines, the matter-antimatter reaction will be able to punch out and destroy the entire pod. The field must be uniform and totally symmetrical."

"Now I know as much as I did before I asked," grumbled McCoy.

"Scotty," spoke up Kirk. "Can you adjust it?"

"Aye, Captain. Heather's got the touch to do the fine adjustin' after I take care of the initial configuration. The only problem's gonna come when the flow starts. The slightest bit off and . . ." His words trailed off. There wasn't any need for him to spell it out. If Scotty failed to make the proper adjustments prior to energy flow being restored, they were all goners.

In silence they waited. Eventually Scott said, "Ready to try it? Good. Spock, give me one paircent flow."

"One percent flow now." The science officer watched his instruments and made minute adjustments. Lights began flashing on the engineering board. Chekov hurried over and, hands shaking slightly and sweat dripping from his face, reached out to press the large red button.

"Energy level reached," the young ensign reported. The tension faded from his face, a smile replacing the look of worry and stress.

"How's it doing, Scotty?"

"A bit more fiddlin', sair. There. Have it. Spock, give me another four paircent."

The slow escalation of power continued until they hit twenty percent; then alarms rang.

"Scotty!" yelled Kirk.

"Radiation leakin' from a thin spot in the bottle. Heather's workin' on it. She . . . she needs help." The radiation scrambled the rest of the engineer's words. On the viewscreen a tiny figure jetted toward the far end of the matter-antimatter pod. The two suited figures merged and became indistinct.

"Radiation level is increasing," reported Spock in a clear, level voice. "Mr. Scott, Chief McConel, return to the protection of the shields."

"Negative," came the faint response. "Gotta do it now or never. Will start chain reaction . . . don't try. Now!"

"Fluctuating power. Swings running eighty percent RMS values. Ask permission to shut down, Captain."

"No, Spock. Let it run for a few seconds more."

"It'll destroy the ship. Scott and McConel cannot possibly have survived the surge."

"I trust Scotty. I trust him."

"Sir, power's leveling at twenty-three percent," reported Chekov. "The fluctuations are gone. Stabilizer circuit is working now."

Kirk heaved a deep sigh. "Scotty, are you there?"

"Aye, Captain. Had a mite of a problem, but we worked it through. Heather's tunin' the dilithium crystal for proper resonance now."

"When will we be up to full warp power?"

"Hard to say, Captain. We still need to do the complete restart. This is just checkin' out the bottles."

"The Rotsler technique for warm restart of the engines is untried, Captain."

"Mr. Spock, I've just seen miracles worked out there. What's another one? I'm sure Mr. Scott can bring us to full power, whether this procedure works or not."

Within forty hours, the *Enterprise* had powered up to full warp capability. Within fifty, Sulu laid in a course for Ammdon.

# Chapter Eleven

*Captain's Log*, Stardate 5011.1

The run to Ammdon was anything but routine. Mr. Scott performed services above and beyond the call of duty maintaining the warp engines. The condition of the MHD bottles is, at best, dangerous. He and his staff will receive commendations for their superb efforts. The remainder of the crew slowly returns to normal, with only occasional relapses attesting to the power of Lorelei's persuasiveness and sonic-laden words. Dr. McCoy assures me no one remains totally under the spell and that all show remarkably stable psycho-trace patterns, considering the rigors they have been through. Lorelei remains in her detention cell, unable to speak directly with anyone. And, in spite of everyone falling back into line, one major obstacle remains: the Ammdon-Jurnamoria peace talks. Without Ambassador Zarv and his diplomatic team, chances are slim that we can prevent the war. However, it is our duty as a Federation vessel to do all we can to avert this war and hold the Romulans at bay in the Orion Arm.

"Status report on the ships around us, Mr. Chekov."

"Captain, I do not know what to make of them. All warships. All heavily armed."

"Spock, comments?"

"Only that this armada is capable of destroying us. Even with the warp engines running at eighty percent full power, we must hold our energy use to a minimum. Use of power for the deflector shields might initiate instability in the magnetic bottles."

"War, Mr. Spock, is what we were sent to stop." James T. Kirk stared at the viewscreen. Moving dots showed the shifting patterns of warships in the Ammdon system. The Jurnamorians had come to the peace talks with most of their navy, it appeared. The Ammdons weren't taking it lightly; most of their fleet, more primitive than that of Jurnamoria but more numerous, maintained defensive positions to prevent mass bombardment of their home. The positions were well chosen, Kirk saw. Both sides had admirals of surpassing ability. In any confrontation there would be tremendous loss of life on both sides.

"Any way of defusing this powder keg?" asked McCoy, peering over his shoulder. Kirk turned and looked back at the doctor.

"Hardly. Turning back such large fleets isn't done in the blink of an eye. They'd also need a reason to return to their home bases."

"What are you going to do, now that Zarv and the others are gone?"

"That is something I haven't figured out yet, Bones. Suggestions? No? Mr. Spock, any ideas?"

"Sir, we ought to beam down to the surface and do what we can. I advise such a move be taken soon. I detect many aboard the Jurnamorian vessels priming their space cannon. Even if no direct order to fire is given, accidents do happen."

"And an accident can cause a war as easily as a direct command. Very well. Bones—you, Uhura, Spock and I will beam down. Mr. Scott is still in the engine room, I take it?"

"He is, sir," came Sulu's quick reply.

"Very well. Mr. Sulu, you have the conn. If anything happens which is not of an engineering nature, get Scotty up here on the double. Otherwise, keep a close lookout on us. Beam us up if the situation merits it."

"Do you think it will, sir?" asked the Oriental.

Kirk heaved a deep sigh and rose to his feet. "I hope not. But my skills as negotiator aren't as sharp as they are in command. I doubt either side will allow me to order them to cease and desist."

He motioned with his head toward the turboelevator and got the small band of officers together to beam down.

"Is he trying to be obtuse, sir?" asked Uhura. The Bantu woman worked the translation computer to give all from the *Enterprise* precise rendering of the rhetoric. "He talks in circles. It is *not* my computer's fault that it comes out gibberish."

"I know, Uhura. Calm down. Diplomacy seems to be ninety-nine percent hot air and one percent insanity."

"I'd argue the point and change it around, Jim," mumbled

McCoy. "There's more insanity in this room than you can shake a stick at."

"While I see no functional value in doing as Dr. McCoy indicated, I do agree with his evaluation of the situation," said Spock. "No amount of talk will sway either side."

"But I've got to give it a try." Kirk rose to his feet, signaled for the privilege of speaking and was recognized by the moderator of the shouting match—Kirk could never call it a debate. It took several seconds for the echoes to die down in the immense room. The Ammdon chambers of state stretched for hundreds of meters. The high-arched roof gave the room the feel of a cathedral, and the coldness of the air added to that impression. The intricately carved wooden table held not only the sundry rubble of papers, portfolios and analyzing devices but also a fair number of small heating units to keep diplomatic hands free of frost-bite. The Ammdon chambers had never been heated; no matter that the middle of winter gripped this side of the planet, the Council of Ammdon did not alter tradition by bringing in warmth.

In a way, Kirk thought this ironic. The words were heated and the mood icy.

He looked up and down the table. The vice-regent of Ammdon had seated the *Enterprise* officers midway along the table. To Kirk's right sat the vice-regent and his staff. To the left were Jurnamoria's Constable of Peace and her half-dozen advisers. Kirk surreptitiously adjusted a throat microphone Spock had bollixed together out of one of the communicators. The others had come prepared for the primitive conditions in the chamber; he hadn't known to come with an amplifier.

"Vice-Regent, Constable, we talk much and accomplish little. The issues dividing your two great worlds," he said, trying not to smile as McCoy muttered sotto voce, "Hogwash," and succeeding, "are not insurmountable."

"Wrong." "He knows nothing!" came the comments, much louder than McCoy's indignant snort.

Kirk held up his hand and got the silence he wanted. He knew instantly the silence wasn't accompanied by open minds.

"We of the Federation have proposed a peace plan which benefits both Ammdon and Jurnamoria. We offer the technical expertise to aid your ailing food industries, and there will be further financial assistance to build new industries. With your planets' drive and personnel and the Federation's vast wealth and knowledge, we can forge a new tomorrow. We can go forward arm in arm toward a future filled with prosperity—and peace."

"Pretty words," snapped the Jurnamorian Constable of Peace. She sneered as she said, "What you offer Jurnamoria is nothing. Nothing! We do not need to be under the heel of alien aggressors. All we need is to have what is rightfully ours—and which *they* have stolen!" She stood and dramatically pointed at the vice-regent.

"There can be no off-planet ownership of Ammdon farmland," said the vice-regent in a polar voice. "And there will be no kowtowing to off-planet dictators!"

"Sir, Lady, please!" pleaded Kirk. It availed him nothing. The two threw insults back and forth until Kirk simply sat down to let them get it out of their systems.

"It was a nice speech, sir," said Uhura. "Even if they didn't listen."

"Thanks. I found it in Zarv's quarters. I wonder how much better he could have delivered it."

"Not much better, Captain," said Spock in a low voice. "My tricorder readings show intense agitation. A motion to adjourn until both sides reconsider and calm themselves would be in order."

Kirk nodded, rose to demand the floor again. What he heard froze him stiff with fear.

"Jurnamorian bitch! Your warships are nothing compared to the might of the Federation vessel circling our planet." The vice-regent's smile turned into a sneer. "The pact with the Federation demands their full defense of Ammdon. Take your fleet and return to your miserable hellhole planet."

Uhura's computer gave a startled yelp as the Constable of Peace answered her Ammdon counterpart. The insult she gave had no direct translation.

". . . we leave now. We shall see how this vaunted defense treaty stands. I think they are cowards. They will not fight. They will turn tail and run, leaving your rotten carcass in the sun for buzzards to pick over."

"It would seem, Captain," said Spock, "that a motion to adjourn is superfluous."

"You have such a powerful grasp of the human condition that it amazes me, Spock," answered McCoy. The group from the *Enterprise* watched as the Jurnamorian constable of peace and her entourage stormed out of the chamber. The angry clicking of their bootheels filled the long, stone-walled room for long minutes after the Jurnamorians had vanished from sight.

"You see how it is, Captain Kirk?" asked the vice-regent. "So bullheaded. Refuses to even consider our side."

"Vice-Regent Falda, your approach needs polishing."

"I think not," the man said, his voice turning from silk to ice.

"Ambassador Zarv's untimely death no doubt contributed to the problems here today, but we require more freedom to prepare. Our subspace radio message to Starbase One will bring another qualified team in a month or so."

"A month? Hardly, Captain Kirk. With Jurnamoria's fleet about our planet, we would not survive a month."

"A cease-fire can last indefinitely until a formal agreement is reached," Kirk said, grasping at straws. "If they withdraw to twenty AUs, will that satisfy you? With the detection equipment supplied by the Federation, this is adequate distance for you to spot a preemptive strike."

"No."

"The *Enterprise* will not fight Ammdon's battles, Vice-Regent Falda. We remain neutral if you initiate hostilities."

Spock's communicator bleeped loudly. He turned to Kirk as he closed the device, saying, "I don't believe Ammdon will initiate battle, Captain."

"Why not?"

"Mr. Sulu reports that the Jurnamorian fleet has fired upon the *Enterprise*."

Kirk raced to the bridge, trailing his other officers behind like the contrail of a rocket plunging through atmosphere. Scotty had assumed command as soon as Sulu saw the Jurnamorian preparations to fire on the *Enterprise*.

"Report, Scotty."

"'Tis nae so bad, sair," he said. "The weapons they use canna penetrate our deflector shields, even at half power. But I kenna if we can fight and maintain deflectors. The fluctuations in the magnetic bottle are worsenin'."

"Danger?"

"Aye, Captain, if it continues much longer."

"Return to engineering and do what you can to keep things held together. I will not be using the phasers unless it is absolutely necessary, but I'll require full deflector screen before we're out of this."

"It'll be touch 'n' go, sair."

"I have every confidence in you, Scotty."

"Aye, sair." The engineer returned to his precious engines to keep them running as smoothly as possible to power the *Enterprise* for the fight slowly building all around.

"Sir, the Ammdon ships have returned fire. See?" The forward viewscreen detailed the burgeoning battle. At first, only a few traces indicated rocket fire between vessels. Then all of space lit like an RR Lyrae star as more of the warcraft launched their barrages. It quickly became impossible for the eye to differentiate between Ammdon and Jurnamorian ships.

"Spock, deflectors up to seventy-five percent full power."

"Powering up now, sir."

Kirk sat, chin in cupped hand, as he thought furiously. If the *Enterprise* so much as fired a single round of photon torpedoes, the battle might be over. And Jurnamoria would be permanently in the Romulan camp. The few remaining crippled vessels would radio back to their home planet and report in full, if they hadn't already indicated that the *Enterprise* took part in the battle.

"Sir, do you want me to prepare a course to warp free of the planet?" asked Sulu.

"We can't run."

"We can't stay and fight, either," spoke up McCoy. "This ship is too much for any of them—any thousand of them."

"I know. Even if we use the phasers at low power, we can blow most of them out of the sky. Technologically, both planets are hundreds of years behind us."

"Only if you measure technological development as the ability to kill," argued McCoy. "What are you going to do, Jim? Lorelei was right, you know. Instead of us preventing a war, we set it off."

"It would have been different if Zarv and Lorritson and Mek Jokkor had been conducting the negotiations."

"I beg to differ, Captain," said Spock. "I recorded the

entire proceedings and submitted them to detailed computer analysis. The situation had progressed too far for anyone to sway either party. The vice-regent's motives are remarkably like those Lorelei outlined. Likewise, the Constable of Jurnamoria refused to listen because of her antipathy to the vice-regent."

"Perhaps a conference with the individual parties," mused Kirk. "Instead of together we ought to have met separately, laid the foundations for a peaceful settlement, then met."

"Such is moot. There are no fewer than six warcraft firing upon us. The deflector screens are holding; however, a notable magnetic flux is being established in the warp-engine MHD bottles."

"Are the dilithium crystals holding? The instability isn't going to crack them?" Without the dilithium crystals, the entire exciter stabilizer circuit failed and the precious magnetic bottles collapsed. The *Enterprise* would either be dead in space again or in peril of exploding in one cataclysmic eruption of matter and antimatter.

"At this point, they are in no danger. If other Jurnamoria ships join the attack against us, I cannot say what the effects will be."

"Should I return fire, sir?" Chekov asked eagerly. His finger quivered over the firing button that would allow incomprehensibly potent phaser beams to leap forth.

"Keep the power at a minimum on the phasers. Ready photon torpedoes. Set proximity fuses to explode one thousand kilometers in front of each target."

"Sir, that will do no damage!"

"Mr. Chekov, your bloodthirstiness in pursuit of defending this ship is admirable, but I don't want to destroy that fleet. I want to show them what we can do—and haven't done."

"Sir," the young ensign said, chastised.

"That's not gonna work, Jim," said McCoy in exasperation. "They'll think we're not destroying them because we can't. When a planet gets the warring bloodlust like they've got it, nothing but victory or death will sate it."

"Mr. Chekov, are torpedo triggers set as ordered?"

"Aye, sir."

"Fire tubes four through seven—now!"

Chekov's finger plunged downward savagely. A deep shudder passed through the ship as the four photon torpedoes launched. On the viewscreen the torpedo traces showed vividly in comparison to the smaller, less effective rockets fired by the warring craft. The screen turned blinding white as the four torpedoes exploded a million meters in front of their targets.

"Sir, they're renewing their attack. Three of the craft we fired on are disabled. They are forming on us and allowing the Ammdon vessels free rein."

"Scotty, give me impulse power to get out of orbit. Let's try to lead them away from Ammdon, if nothing else."

The vessel quivered as power flooded the ignition chambers of the impulse engines. Kirk knew he risked much with this maneuver. Fuel for the impulse engines was at a premium; using the warp power would have been a more conservative approach, but he worried at the instabilities mounting in the stardrive engines. If he needed phaser power, it had to come from their gargantuan energy reserves available, even at an eighty percent functional level.

"They are following us, sir. Their communications officers are tracking and giving course data," reported Uhura. "There isn't too much else being passed between them."

"They know what to do. This is a warlike culture. They've practiced enough to act without overt direction." Kirk sat back and enjoyed the brief respite he'd won by turning tail and running.

"Sir, the vice-regent wishes to speak to you. He sounds very angry."

"I imagine he is, Lieutenant. Very well, put him on the screen." Kirk watched as the viewscreen tore apart, then re-formed with the image of Vice-Regent Falda. The man's chocolate complexion had turned even darker with anger. Kirk imagined he saw sparks actually flitting about in the jet irises as Falda tried in vain to control his wrath.

"Captain Kirk," he said, turning the name into an insult. "You run like a whipped cur. You throw Ammdon to the wolves at our door. What value is this Federation of yours if it does not deliver the protection our treaty guarantees?"

"Vice-Regent, greetings." Kirk waited for the man to respond. When he didn't, Kirk smiled and said mildly, "We have no wish to be caught between warring factions. We do not wish to view this war at all. We bring offers of peace, of assistance."

"Assistance means helping us destroy those interlopers! They bombard my planet even at this moment. We outnumber them, but their weapons are superior to ours. We require your firepower to stop them. Without it, we perish."

"Jim," whispered McCoy. "Should you contact Starfleet and get orders?"

"It wouldn't do any good. I know as much about the situation as anyone there—more. If I can't handle it, how can a bureaucrat four hundred parsecs away?"

Kirk held up his hand to silence McCoy. "I won't pass along the responsibility, Bones. This is my command. I've been assigned to keep the peace, and I'll do it. I will!"

"Captain Kirk, are you returning to defend Ammdon, or do we count this as a breaching of the Ammdon-Federation treaty?" The vice-regent glared from the viewscreen.

"We will return, Vice-Regent Falda. As long as your ships do not fire on us, as they were doing."

"The heat of battle," the man apologized insincerely. "Our peace-loving commanders lack experience. Some fired at anything in their sights."

"I'm sure that's how it happened. However, there is a condition to our return. We will once more sit at the conference table and discuss mutually acceptable *peaceful* solutions to your problems with Jurnamoria."

"Sit with Constable Ganessa? Impossible. She ordered this attack. I have no truck with murderers."

"I'm sure she'd say the same, Captain," said Spock. "Their bioprofiles indicate extreme hostility toward one another. If Ammdon or Jurnamoria had selected any other negotiators, this might have been avoided. The personality conflicts are too great."

"They're too much alike," said Kirk, nodding in understanding and still at a loss how to defuse the interplanetary war and all its far-reaching consequences.

A flare of red lights caught Kirk's attention. All over the bridge flashed emergency warnings. The deflector screens at full barely held off the attacks launched against them now.

"Phasers, sir? More torpedoes?" Chekov nervously licked his lips, eyes riveted to the readouts showing how near the point of failure for the screens was.

"More power to the deflectors." He thought hard. if they turned and ran, they might reach starbase before everything aboard the *Enterprise* fell apart or blew up. But that accomplished nothing. The war would rage between Ammdon and Jurnamoria, and the Romulans would have what they wanted: a planetary civil war that they could exploit for their own expansionist motives. If the *Enterprise* fought, the Jurnamorian fleet might be destroyed and Jurnamoria must align with the Romulans as a self-defense measure. There seemed no way to defeat either fleet without massive loss of life, since the leaders were totally opposed to further negotiations.

"Spock, identify the flagship with Constable of Peace Ganessa aboard."

"Done, sir. Her vessel is at distance seventeen point zero light-seconds, heading—"

"Never mind all that. Sulu, maneuver us closer. Maintain deflectors at full power. Mr. Chekov, use photon torpedoes to keep them as far away as possible. Try to interdict incoming rockets with our phasers, set on lowest power."

"What is it you're planning, sir?" asked Spock.

"Prepare the transporter, Mr. Spock. I want to get close enough to the constable's flagship to beam her out. And at the same time I want the *Enterprise* positioned in such a way that we can beam up the vice-regent."

"But you can't do that, Jim. Their deflector shields'd prevent it," protested McCoy.

"You're forgetting something, Bones. These are primitive ships. They don't have deflectors."

"They have to."

"No, sir," said Sulu. "None does. I never thought of it before the captain mentioned it. We're too used to fighting ships at the same technological level."

"So, all right, you beam the two leaders aboard. Then what? They still hate one another."

"Dr. McCoy, your lack of faith in me is appalling. I think I see a way of resolving many of our problems with one small meeting of the minds."

McCoy shook his head. Scotty burst onto the bridge and cried, "The engines'll take nae more, Captain. The deflector shields are wearin' us down too much."

"Cut power forty percent as you use the transporter."

"Transporter?" he cried in surprise. "But, Captain, that's nae possible. I kenna be sure we'll hold together or not."

"Do it, on Spock's command. Mr. Spock?"

"Nearing locus, sir. Approximately equidistant between Ammdon's surface and the Jurnamorian flagship *Bor*. Transporter room, activate now!"

The lights dimmed on the bridge as power shifted from internal demands to the transporter. As soon as the enormous energy requirements of the transporter had been met, Kirk ordered full deflector screens and a course away from Ammdon.

"Put us out of reach of both fleets. I want *this* peace conference to be uninterrupted."

He swung out of his seat and motioned for Spock and McCoy to accompany him. Dr. McCoy followed, grumbling. The expression on Spock's face was unreadable.

# Chapter Twelve

*Captain's Log,* Stardate 5012.5

I find my ship to be in jeopardy. The intense assault by the Jurnamorian fleet has severely damaged certain portions of the *Enterprise*. Mr. Scott and his able staff are repairing those circuits most needed for warp-speed capability. I have ordered beamed aboard the Ammdon and Juramorian leaders for one final conference. There is one last tactic I have not tried to bring peace to the warring planets. If it fails, I must return to Starbase One and allow the Romulans their way with this section of space. I do not think I will fail this time. My argument for peace is one so potent the vice-regent of Ammdon and the Constable of Peace of Jurnamoria will not be able to resist.

"I protest this cavalier behavior on your part, Captain Kirk," Vice-Regent Falda said in his icy tones. "Your technology was to aid, not to kidnap. I demand to be returned to my planet immediately. The war raging requires my personal supervision."

To one side of the transporter room stood Constable of Peace Ganessa, arms crossed just below her small breasts. She glared at all and said nothing until Spock tried to take her arm and escort her into the corridor. The woman flew into a murderous rage, slamming Spock back against a bulkhead.

"She is remarkably strong, Captain. I had not anticipated such strength in the Jurnamorians."

"Try to touch me again, deformed one, and I'll show you Jurnamorian strength."

"You won't be harmed, Constable. I give you my word," said Kirk.

"Your word? What's that? The promise of one bedding with Ammdons? A kidnapper? How did you steal me away from the safety of my vessel? The *Bor* is the strongest vessel in space, yet no alarm was raised when your boarding party entered."

"Entered?" asked McCoy, puzzled.

"You must have used some diabolical gas to poison my crew, then whisked me away and brought me here."

"Was she unconscious at any time, Mr. Kyle?" asked McCoy, concerned for her health. "A blow to the head might have distorted both time and perception."

"Doc, she arrived in one piece and fighting mad. I don't know what she's carrying on about."

"Vice-Regent, Constable, please accompany me. Since you seem unwilling to do so at my personal request, as the captain of this ship I hereby order you to do so." A security team, phasers drawn, appeared. "Please escort our guests to the detention level."

"Detention level?" parroted Falda. "So you imprison me. I will petition that the Ammdon-Federation treaty be voided because of this discourtesy. Or, if you slay me, my successor will so order."

"See the type of slime lizard you bed with, Falda?" taunted Ganessa. "They are as treacherous as the Romulans claimed."

"I mistrusted the Romulans; their motives were too transparent. But perhaps I was hasty. They might have been turned to Ammdon's advantage, after all."

"They are Jurnamoria's advantage now, scum eater." The woman stalked off, head held high. Falda cast Kirk a withering look and followed at a discreet distance, close enough to watch Ganessa but far enough back to thwart any attack she might launch.

When the security team and their two hostages vanished into the turboelevator, McCoy took Kirk's arm and spun him around. "What's the meaning of this, Jim? You can't hold the heads of two planets like this. That's a violation of—"

"Noninterference with a culture's right to self-determination. I'm aware of that. But what I'm going to do is meddling even more. I have to count on a peaceful settlement so that neither side will want to tell Starfleet exactly what's happened up to this point."

"They'll hang you, Jim, and the entire crew along with you. I don't have any desire to see my neck stretched."

"You are quite right, Doctor," broke in Spock, coming down the stairwell from above. "Your neck is already quite long enough. Further elongation would give you the aspect of one of your planet's turkeys."

Kirk gripped the doctor's arm and squeezed so that he

wouldn't respond to Spock's sarcasm. To Spock he said, "Is the detention cell ready for our guests?"

"Eminently so, Captain. I wish you luck with this ploy."

"I didn't think you believed in luck, Mr. Spock."

"I don't, Captain. But it is obvious you do, or you'd never have tried such a scheme."

"Let's go to the detention level. I want to see how things are progressing." The turboelevator returned and the trio entered. The lift speedily deposited them on the level above. Before entering the cell area, Spock took earplugs from his pocket and handed them to both Kirk and McCoy while inserting a pair into his own ears.

"What are these for?" asked McCoy.

"I had Mr. Spock construct them specially for our use. They filter out all but the frequencies between two hundred fifty and two thousand hertz."

"That's about the normal range for human voices."

"They filter out harmonics and beats and other interesting but virtually unexplored areas of speech. What you hear will sound flat and even uninteresting, but the reason for the earplugs will be obvious."

Kirk gestured for his two friends to enter the detention area. Mr. Neal stood by, earplugs already in place. Inside the large cell where Lorelei had been alone, she now had two visitors. Neither the vice-regent of Ammdon nor the Constable of Peace of Jurnamoria appeared to enjoy the small woman's company in the least.

"We must protest, Kirk. This is a violation of the Covenants of War. You cannot imprison three in one cell of this size."

"Especially when two are leaders," cut in the vice-regent, glaring at Ganessa.

"It seems you've already found one area for agreement.

You don't want to remain in this cell longer than necessary. I don't think you will be here for much longer."

"Let us out. Now." The cut of command laced the constable's voice.

"Shortly." To Lorelei he said, "A word in private, please." The small woman stood by Kirk, her hand rising to touch the earplugs he wore. She made no attempt to remove them.

"You trust me so little?" she asked.

"Lorelei, you can only be true to your philosophy, what you've trained for all your life as a Speaker of Hyla. I don't ask any more. Unless you wish to allow a war to rage, one which you all too accurately predicted."

"The presence of your ship precipitated the war?" she asked. Kirk only nodded. The woman's words echoed slightly, sounding flat and almost lifeless due to the earplugs. Only the intensity of her personality acted on him—or was it also her pheromones to which he was so intimately attuned? Even with the earplugs, Jim Kirk had to fight to keep from falling under this beguiling woman's spell.

"I wish I found some satisfaction in saying 'I told you so.' That particular idiom is new to me, but it fits so many of your situations. On Hyla, there is scant opportunity for such words. We know our destiny and all contribute to achieving it."

"There's nothing more I can do with either Ganessa or Falda. Would you talk to them? Just for a few minutes? Try to persuade them that their war is a foolish one and that they really ought to cooperate."

"I will see what can be done, but I will not speak for your Federation."

"Speak for peace. That's what we both want in the matter."

She nodded briskly. The tiredness washed from her face and the woman turned to the others in the cell. Where once she had felt the strain of influencing an entire starship crew of the error of their ways, now she had only two. Lorelei began talking, first in Hylan, then in the common language shared by Ammdon and Jurnamoria.

Kirk stood by Spock and McCoy as the woman began learning more and more of the Ammdon speech.

"It is truly amazing, Captain, how fast she learns a language. Lorelei not only picks up the gross grammar, she seems to intuitively understand the nuances."

"The body language is part of it. Look at that," said McCoy. "See how she lifts her left shoulder and drops her right when she speaks to Ganessa? That must have something to do with obeisance, of knowing her position."

"Knowing her position," said Kirk, smiling. "Falda and Ganessa haven't seen the smallest part of what Lorelei can do. She's just now mastering their language."

"It took four point nine three minutes," offered Spock.

"In just about five minutes she's dickering with them, probing, finding their weaknesses. In another ten, she'll have them shaking hands." Kirk felt the vibrancy of Lorelei's voice, even through the earplugs. He watched as she positively radiated confidence as she expounded on the True Path, on peace and mutual cooperation. Like magic, the frowns and tenseness faded from both Ganessa and Falda, to be replaced with a wariness of one another. Soon this too vanished and the lifelong antagonists began arguing, not with rancor but for mutual gain. Threats no longer entered their speech as they bargained for the maximum possible for their individual worlds.

"It's truly amazing," said McCoy. "Those two act like business partners rather than commanders of opposing armies. Why, I can actually *feel* it when Lorelei talks to them. She must be laying on the sonic persuasion as heavily as she can."

"I'm certain of it. Note the expression as her empathic powers sense the shifts in mood. Two enemies are becoming two cautious friends. And, unless I miss my guess, Falda and Ganessa are strong enough leaders to sway their own people. They'll return to Ammdon and Jurnamoria with peace plans instead of war tactics. And they'll make it stick, in spite of the hawks that must have surrounded them for so many years."

Satisfied, James Kirk indicated that Lorelei and the two leaders be left alone to work out any remaining differences. The only thing he misjudged was the time it took Lorelei to convince Ganessa and Falda to shake hands. It wasn't ten minutes; it was eight.

"I'm undecided as to what to do with Lorelei," Kirk admitted to Spock. The captain of the *Enterprise* hiked tired feet up and put them on the corner of the desk as he leaned back in his seat. His quarters provided about the only sanctuary he had now. The crew bustled about, repairing all they could to prepare for the long trip back to Starbase One. Lorelei had achieved great results with Ganessa and Falda, but their respective cabinets refused to support peaceful actions—until they, too, had the opportunity to speak with Lorelei.

"She is not technically a Federation citizen," Spock pointed out. "Therefore, she cannot act as Federation ambassador."

"I'm not too worried about that. We can come up with some high-sounding title. Representative or counselor-at-large or delegate without portfolio. Anything to make it sound official. That's the small part of it. What I don't know about is her effect on Ammdon and Jurnamoria."

"She will not turn them against us. Not as long as she follows her so-called True Path."

"But, Spock," cried Kirk, dropping his feet to the deck and leaning forward over the desk, "we've got to think about the Romulans. They won't leave the planets alone if they get wind of any pacifist tendencies. They'll swoop in and take them as neat as wolves going after lambs."

"Your metaphor smacks of Dr. McCoy."

"It's nonetheless something to consider."

"Perhaps we can let the Romulans know that the Federation will not tolerate intervention in this system."

Kirk shook his head. "If Lorelei has her way in this system—and she will—how do we keep the Romulans out?"

A faint upturning at the corners of Spock's lips made Kirk more attentive. Something amused his science officer. Whatever it was, it had to be of the highest magnitude.

"What is it, Spock?"

"An idea crossed my mind, Captain. Do you suppose it is possible to arrange for Lorelei to be kidnapped by the Romulans?"

"Kidnapped! Why, they'd—" Kirk stopped, then laughed. "They wouldn't kill her. They would end up being the challenge of her life. Stopping a war between two backward planets would be like child's play for her compared to the efforts required to turn the Romulans into peaceful beings."

"It might not be practical, but it is something worth thinking about, Captain."

"You're right, Spock. And until that comes up, she can maintain the peace better than anyone. I can see the day when the ones like Zarv and Lorritson are out of jobs, all Federation negotiating being done by Hylans."

"That is assuming they can stand Federation policy. To them, we must be intensely warlike."

"You're a Vulcan. Can you pass up the challenge of

convincing a Hylan we're not, that we seek only peace but are ready to fight to prevent a greater violence?"

"No, Captain, I cannot pass up such a challenge. And neither can you."

"So right, Mr. Spock. Let's inform all those concerned of the decision."

Whistling, and noticing it was flat because of the earplugs he still wore, Jim Kirk smiled. It wouldn't be much longer before the earplugs weren't needed aboard the *Enterprise*.

"Is this agreeable to all concerned?" Kirk asked.

"Lorelei is acceptable to the people of Jurnamoria," said Ganessa, Constable of Peace.

"To those of Ammdon, also." Falda hesitated, then added, "There are some points of dissension we must work out. Lorelei has accepted the task of dealing with those for us."

"Good." Turning to the viewscreen, now directed at the detention cell where Lorelei was still quartered to provide filtering capability for her sonic brainwashing, Kirk said, "You realize, Lorelei, that you do not officially represent the Federation?"

"That is my wish. I do not represent Hyla, either, although I am a Speaker. This is a personal mission."

"As such, the Federation can send an ambassador at a later date to work out the terms of a trade pact between all parties."

"It is expected," said Vice-Regent Falda. "Lorelei has convinced us that interchange between our cultures will be mutually beneficial."

Kirk hid his surprise. If Lorelei said such a thing, she had motives of her own. Perhaps free run of Federation worlds, spreading her True Path philosophy, might be guaranteed if she applied for entry as a representative of Ammdon and Jurnamoria. He didn't much care. That sort of thing was for diplomats and politicians to worry over. He had carried out his orders and stopped the war. For the time being, the Romulan thrust through the Orion Arm had been halted.

"I need some further information from Lorelei before beaming her to Ammdon."

"What is this, James?" she asked quietly. For the first time, he felt no twinge of sonic lacing in her words. They carried no persuasive undercurrents but only simple curiosity.

"We have no way of contacting Hyla with news of your survival. That explosion aboard your ship prevented your communications officer from doing more than broadcasting a simple SOS. Any information you have on how we might go about finding Hyla would be appreciated."

She studied Kirk for a moment, then smiled. "Before, I might have been reluctant. You *are* warlike, but you are learning. Yes, I will give you what information I can so you can seek out Hyla."

For a moment neither spoke; then Kirk broke the silence. "We'll meet again, Lorelei. I'm sure of it."

"I, too, James. We'll meet once more on happier terms."

The viewscreen switched off. Kirk heaved himself out of the command seat and said to his two guests, "Mr. Spock will see you to the transporter room and beam you back to Ammdon. If there is anything you need, please feel free to contact the Federation."

But Ganessa and Falda barely heard. They nodded curtly and left, heads together, shoulders rubbing, speaking in low voices. Spock followed them into the turboelevator.

"Now, there goes a happy couple," said McCoy.

"Hmm, oh, they're just discussing . . . treaties," said Kirk, eyes twinkling.

"You're starting to sound like Spock. Those two are in love. Imagine, hating one another for so long, and now, who knows?"

"Yes, Doctor, who knows." Turning to Sulu, he requested operational status.

"Transporter activated. Ganessa, Falda and Lorelei beamed down."

"Very good, Mr. Sulu. Lay in a course for Starbase One. Mr. Scott," Kirk called out. "Would you feel put upon if I asked for warp factor one?"

"I canna guarantee the engines, sair, but they can take warp factor one for a few weeks."

"Excellent. Lay in course for home, Mr. Sulu. Warp factor one."

All seemed right to James T. Kirk now. The crew had returned to its normal efficiency, all was at peace and the mission, in spite of serious setbacks, had been successfully completed.

The *Enterprise* shivered with power, then leaped from orbit on a direct line for Starbase One, refitting and a much-needed rest for both equipment and crew.

The Novel STAR TREK® Fans
Have Waited Twenty Years For...

**STAR TREK®**

# SPOCK'S WORLD

**by**
**Diane Duane**

Ever since 1966, when the very first episode of the original STAR TREK television series aired, casual fans and devoted Trekkers alike have been captivated by the alien Mr. Spock and his home planet Vulcan.

Now, for the first time anywhere, you can have an in-depth look at both.

**SPOCK'S WORLD...**
A September 1988 Hardcover Release
from Pocket Books.



110

THE
STAR TREK
PHENOMENON